Island of the
Great Yellow Ox

Island of the Great Yellow Ox

Walter Macken

SIMON & SCHUSTER BOOKS FOR YOUNG READERS

Published by Simon & Schuster

New York • London • Toronto • Sydney • Tokyo • Singapore

SIMON & SCHUSTER BOOKS FOR YOUNG READERS
Simon & Schuster Building, Rockefeller Center
1230 Avenue of the Americas, New York, New York 10020
SIMON & SCHUSTER BOOKS FOR YOUNG READERS
is a trademark of Simon & Schuster Inc.

Designed by Lucille Chomowicz.
The text of this book is set in 11.5 Point Janson.
Manufactured in the United States of America. 10 9 8 7 6 5 4 3 2 1

Library of Congress Cataloging-in-Publication Data: Macken, Walter.
Island of the great yellow ox / Walter Macken 1915—1967. p.   cm.
Summary: A terrifying storm washes Conor, his little brother,
and two American friends up on to Ox Island where they become
prisoners of the eccentric Lady Agnes who will stop at nothing
to uncover the Druid Treasure.
    [1. Adventure and adventurers—Fiction.   2. Buried treasure—
Fiction.   3. Islands—Fiction.]   I. Title. PZ7.M198Is   1991
[Fic]—dc20   90-22515 CIP AC   ISBN 0-671-73800-3

Island of the
Great Yellow Ox

chapter

1

Conor came out of his house carefully eating a slice of bread and jam. The jam on the bread was generous since he had put it on out of the jar himself. It was homemade blackberry jam and it tasted very good.

On the road outside the cottage he looked across the bay. The mountains on the far side were blue and misty. The sea between was calm and still.

Their house was down near the seashore and he set off along the little road that would lead him to the main road.

He forgot that his mother and his big brother and sister were in the oat field stacking the ripe oats. He should have gone the other way.

"Conor," his mother called, "where are you off to?"

"Just up the road," he said.

"Have you done all the housework?" she asked.

"Yes," he said.

"Well, don't be too long," she called. "Your father will soon be home from the fair."

"No," he said, thinking that his father always brought a bag of candy home with him when he went to the fair.

"Take Babo with you," she said next.

"I will not," said Conor, "he's a pain in the neck."

"Ah, poor little Babo," she said.

"Poor little Babo, my eye!" said Conor indignantly, and he saw his brother and sister laughing.

"Well, don't be too late," she said.

"I won't, Mother," he said, and then ran in case they might ask him to do anything else.

When he was out of their sight, he stopped running and carefully finished eating the bread and jam. There was a little jam on his fingers and he licked it off.

He stopped on the road above, wondering whether he would go down to the sea sand or along the road to the hotel. He liked both places. He liked the hotel because of all the strange cars and people you could see there in the summer. You could also see a lot of strange people on the beach, since this was August and the weather was fine and sunny.

He decided that he would see both places: he would walk down to the beach and then go back to the hotel along the rocky shore.

He was a little while making this decision, sitting on the stone wall. He could see the whole wide maw of the bay laid out before him like a map, enclosed all around by tall mountains, like a big letter U. The bay held all kinds of small islands and jagged rocks that you couldn't see so well now, when the tide was in. One big island was way out in the Atlantic, and even on this calm day you could see the white water at the foot of its cliffs. There were a few white-sailed pleasure boats on the bay, and a few fishing currachs.

He was rising to go down the narrow rutted road to the beach when some instinct made him turn his head.

There behind him, watching him from the other side of the road, was his brother Babo.

He was a small boy, just four, with very pale hair that was almost white, and a round, pudgy face with red lips. He stood there now in bare feet, with his hands behind his back, looking very innocent.

"Who told you to follow me?" Conor asked.

Babo didn't answer him.

"Go home," said Conor. "I tell you to go home. I don't want you."

Babo didn't say anything.

Look at him, Conor thought, you'd think he was an angel, and he's a little demon.

He bent down and took up three stones from the road.

"If you don't go home," he said. "I'll fire stones at you just like I'd do with a puppy dog."

He knew by the way Babo creased his eyebrows that he was going to be obstinate. Just because he's the youngest, they all have him spoiled, he thought.

He had to fire the stones. Of course, he fired them well

to each side of Babo, but the little fellow closed his eyes and cringed just as if he would be hit, when he knew very well he wouldn't be. If there were anybody watching them, of course they would say: "Look at that cruel boy, throwing stones at his little brother."

So he ran down the rutty lane toward the beach as fast as he could. This was the only way to get away from Babo, because he was too small to have much running in his legs.

It was a long beach of silver-colored sand. There were a lot of people on the sand, mostly children building sandcastles near the water so that the moats would be filled and the castles eventually conquered and toppled by the sea. There were people swimming in the surf, and grown people lying around in swim suits or eating lunch from picnic baskets.

Conor gave them a wide berth. He never got to know those summer people. They were from a different world. If one of them spoke to him, he would become tongue-tied and unable to answer.

He turned his head and saw Babo come panting onto the beach. So he ran again toward the end, where it became very rocky. He knew this would slow Babo up and, if he got a good lead on him, Babo might give up and go home.

For the next half hour he forgot all about him. The stones were very large and black, slippery with seaweed, and he had to travel cautiously. Of course he could have gone farther up to his left and traveled along the coast by the green fields. That way he would only have to climb over a stone wall here and there, but it seemed much more adventurous to clamber over the rocks and imagine that all sorts of things were happening to him.

He was surprised when he topped a rock and saw the inlet below him and a cabin cruiser tied up to the pier.

This inlet was merely a natural cleft between two large rocks. Even at low tide it was deep and well sheltered from the winds. The tops of the rocks at one side had been chipped off and made into a sort of pier with cement. Iron rings had been sunk in the cement to tie up a boat. This had been done many years before by strangers who had come there and were fond of the sea and had built a small cottage back from the bay. He could see the cottage now. It appeared to be empty. The curtains were drawn on the windows. They had heard a few months earlier that it had been bought by a captain and his wife, who had cruised the big bay a lot since they came, landing on islands to explore them, and fishing. People said they were archaeologists, but Conor didn't quite know what that meant. Neither did a lot of other people, but it put a label on the newcomers and thus satisfied nearly everybody.

A daring thought came into his head now.

Since there seemed to be nobody around, why not go down and have a look at the cruiser?

No sooner had the thought come into his head than he acted upon it. He looked around him in all directions and saw no sign of any living thing. He was wearing sandshoes, so his feet made no sound as he climbed the last rocks and then made his way to the path that led from the cottage to the pier. The cruiser was riding high because the tide was in.

It was a white boat. It was decked in front, with a cockpit in the middle where the wheel was for guiding her. It was decked at the back too, and this would contain the sleeping and eating cabin, he thought, and the front place would be the galley. The portholes of the cabins were below the rim of the pier.

He couldn't resist it. He stepped softly onto the boat. It barely rocked to his weight. First he thought he would go into the cockpit and pretend to be driving the boat, then he saw the glass windows on top of the cabin, which were protected by brass rails. This would be the best thing to do—to look down and see what the cruiser was like inside—so he stretched his length on the deck and looked down below.

He was nearly petrified with shock, because he found himself looking down at a table on which was spread a map and a person on each side was bending over the map. He could see their heads. One was the head of an enormous fat man wearing a yachting cap and the other was the head of a woman with white hair. Her finger was tracing a point on the map. It was a big map, drawn on the sort of nearly transparent paper he often saw with engineers or people who were building houses.

He couldn't move. He could hear her voice.

"It has to be here," she was saying. "There is absolutely no other place in the whole bay. This has to be the one. If you compare the tale of Cathbadh and the indications of the hieroglyphics on the great stone, it must be the one. That's the island of the two heads. Look, you can see them. And what is it called now? The Island of the Great Yellow Ox. Even the local people call it Ox Island, so you see how it all ties up with tradition. There is no other one, I tell you. I am satisfied. This is it. After all these years we are at last within sight of our goal."

She had spread her arms and leaned back on the bunk with an air of triumph. This brought her head up, and the next moment Conor found her eyes looking into his.

He couldn't move. He saw alarm come into her eyes, awareness, and then furious anger. It seemed to him that her whole face changed, until he was terrified by the look that appeared in her eyes. Sparks seemed to be shooting out of them, her lips drew back from her yellowed teeth, and she pointed a shaking finger up at him. She shouted, "Look!" and that shout released him. He got up from his position, jumped onto the pier, and ran. He was frightened. She had had an awful look on her face. He didn't know why the sight of him had changed her.

He was going to run up the path to the cottage and around that and up to the road, but he suddenly changed his mind. He guessed how long it would take them to get on the pier, then he ran at the big rock that sheltered it, scrambled up fast, and slid down the other side. Here a few yards beyond he knew where two stones arched together and he made for this, crouched inside, and let the seaweed drape back over the opening to conceal him. He found he was panting hard, so he put his two hands over his mouth and breathed between his fingers.

He heard the sound of their voices then.

"Where is he? Where could he have gone?" This was the woman.

"Miles away by now." He heard the deep voice of the captain. "Are you sure there was some boy there?"

"I'm not blind," he heard her say viciously. "I saw the little monster. We'll have to find him."

"What would he know?" he heard the captain ask. "He only got a look."

"He saw the map, you fool," he heard her say. "How long was he there? We don't know. How much did he hear?"

"He wouldn't know anything about it," the captain said. "It would be all Greek to him."

"Hey, you, little boy," he heard her calling. "Did you see another boy around here with brown hair and blue eyes? You hear me?"

"Agnes, for goodness' sake!" the captain said. "That little fellow would be hardly able to talk. How would he know?"

"Come here to me! Come here to me, little boy!" he heard her say. "Now, look at him. He has run away. Go after him! Ask him!"

"Agnes, for goodness' sake," the captain said. "All you are doing is drawing attention to us. Calm down. The boy saw nothing he would understand. Calm down. Be sensible."

"I'll tell you one thing," he heard her say. "We are going out there now. We are not going to waste any more time. Come on. Get aboard. Let us get out there."

"The glass is going down, you know," he said. "The barometer is very low. I'd say we are in for a big blow."

"Not right away, surely," she said. "We'll have time to get out there. It will take only a couple of hours. We can be there before the storm, can't we?"

"We can if we hurry," he heard the captain say.

Then there was silence. Conor still held his breath, afraid that they would come over the big stone and find his hiding place. In five minutes he heard the throb of powerful engines fading away, and after another few minutes he came out of his hiding place, climbed a bit, and put his head over the rock. He saw the big boat going out and turning left around the Bishop's Rock and making for the tortuous channel that led to the open sea.

He turned his head then. Way up on a far field he saw Babo standing with his hands behind his back. At least he didn't tell them, he thought. That is a mark in his favor. He knew where I must be. Babo traveled by the fields, so he would have been able to look down and see everything.

All the same, he thought, I am still going to lose him.

He came and walked to the path and turned off that into the fields, and set off running again. He decided he would go back to the hotel.

He paused once to look out at the boat, now far away. The sight of it made him shiver. He couldn't understand why. Then he shrugged the whole thing off and began to jog trot toward the hotel, concentrating once again on a way to outwit his brother Babo.

chapter

2

He paused at the back of the hotel where the deliveries were made. There was a sort of a dock filled with boxes and crates and apparent confusion. He wondered at the difference between the front and the back; the front with its neatly graveled drive and clean, gleaming automobiles. He wondered what it would be like to go into the front of the hotel if you were a guest.

He walked on to the green acres behind. These were sand dunes and piled rocks that had gradually been covered with coarse grass that was cropped close by sheep. He leaped over a stream that ran down to the shore and, gaining a green height, he threw himself down on the grass. He could see the whole bay from there, all the rocks and all the islands. Below him men were collecting periwinkles in buckets and filling sacks with them.

He turned and looked inland. It was very hot. There was a kind of mist rising to cloak the sun.

Miles away, it seemed, he saw two people hitting a golf ball. They had only one club. One would hit the ball and as they walked after it the other would take the club and hit it on farther. Shading his eyes against the glare, he saw that they were two boys, one with shorts like himself and the other with long trousers. Wouldn't it be nice, he thought, if they would ask me to join in their game? Not that he would be able to hit a golf ball. He laughed at this thought and then turned on his back and shaded his eyes from the heat.

He heard a thump behind him, and a slither, and the funniest thing happened. He opened his eyes when he felt it and there was a golf ball right on top of his sweater, resting there as if it had been put there by a hand.

He didn't move. If he did the golf ball would have fallen off. He heard the boys' footsteps running toward him, and they were laughing. Then he saw their legs beside him, bare legs with sandshoes on the feet and long, gray-green trouser legs, which were crumpled over blue-and-white high-top sneakers. He must be an American, Conor thought when he saw the shoes.

"Hey, do you mind if I slice the ball from your chest?" he heard the voice say. The boy bent down so that he could see him. He had blond hair cropped very close and blue eyes. He was smiling.

"No," said Conor.

"Fine," he said. He put a leg each side of Conor's body

and swung the club a few times. Conor's stomach contracted with anticipation. I hope he has a good aim, he thought, or he'll cripple me.

Then he heard them laughing and they sat down beside him. Conor raised himself on an elbow and caught the ball as it fell from him.

"Did you really think I would try and hit the ball off you?" the blond boy asked.

"I thought so," said Conor, looking at them. They were about his own age. The other boy was very dark and inclined to be plump. He wore a khaki shirt with his shorts.

"Wasn't it funny that the ball landed on your chest?" this boy asked. "I bet that's bigger odds than a hole in one."

"Do you live around here?" the blond boy asked.

"I do," said Conor," "way behind."

"I'm George," said the blond boy. "This is Edwin. We met in the hotel. What do you do around here?"

"What do you mean?" Conor asked.

"All we do is swim and eat," said George. "What do you do in your free time?"

"Oh," said Conor. "I help my father. We have a farm. He fishes as well."

"What kind of fishing?" Edwin asked.

"Oh, all kinds," said Conor.

"Has he a big trawler?" asked Edwin.

"Oh, no," said Conor, laughing. "A small boat, a currach."

"That's a rowboat," said George. "I've seen them, I guess. Black with a high prow. Do you go out with him often?"

"Sometimes," said Conor.

"That's something I'd do," said Edwin. "We haven't been out on the sea properly at all."

"Does your father own the boat?" George asked.

"Oh, of course he does," said Conor. "He made it."

"Made his own boat!" said Edwin. "My father has a riverboat at home, but he didn't make it. He bought it."

"What's your name?" George asked.

"Conor," he said.

"Well, look, Conor," said George, "how about us having a look at this boat?"

"But it's only a boat," said Conor. "What would you be wanting to see it for?"

"Just to see," said George. "It would pass the time."

"Does he belong to you?" Edwin asked.

"Who?" asked Conor, bewildered.

"That little kid there."

Conor felt his heart sinking. He looked around. About ten yards away was Babo, sitting on the grass like a little Buddha, tossing pebbles in his palm.

"Oh," Conor groaned. "That's my brother. He followed me. I couldn't get rid of him. Don't pay any attention to him."

"He seems all right," said Edwin.

"He's a plague," said Conor.

"I know," said George. "I have one too. He's a jerk.

There should be a law against little brothers."

"Would you really like to see the boat?" Conor asked.

"Love to," said Edwin.

Conor rose to his feet.

"All right so," he said. "We'll go and see it. It's quite a way off."

"We have time," said George.

As they stood there Conor noticed that they were all nearly the same height. George was the tallest. He was thin. Conor was next in height, and Edwin an inch or so under him. He liked them. They were friendly. Wasn't it odd, he thought, how he was wishing they would talk to him and here they were now walking together.

"We can go by the shore or the road," he said. " If we go by the shore we will have a lot of climbing to do."

"That suits me," said George. "We'll go by the shore. That way we might also lose the little brother."

"We might," said Conor, "but I doubt it."

They set off along the shore. Part of it was beach, which was easy to negotiate, but here and there it rose to short cliffs, which they had to climb because the tide was in and they couldn't walk at the foot of them.

But Conor enjoyed it. They searched the clumps of seaweed as they traveled. They found odd things: the square of cork from a fishing net, some oddly shaped stones, a child's broken sand bucket, the skeleton of a big fish—many things that delayed them.

They crossed the long beach, which was becoming empty now, for reasons they didn't stop to think about, and beyond the beach where the shore became rough again, neatly tucked into a little bay sheltered from all the winds, they came on the currach. It was barely floating because the tide was on the turn. It was protected at each side from rock-rubbing by old automobile tires.

And sitting on a rock on the other side, looking at them innocently, was Babo.

"See," said Conor bitterly, "he got around before us. Didn't I tell you he was cunning?"

"Yeah, they're all the same," said George.

Only Edwin looked at the little brother and winked at him. This broke Babo's solemnity and he smiled back. He was pleased that at least one of them didn't look down on him.

Conor showed them how the long boat with the raking prow was built, with canvas stretched and tarred over the slim ribs. It was built for lightness and speed and easy handling. The fishing lines were wound around rectangular wooden frames and tucked away neatly at the sides.

George was looking across the bay. About four miles from them at the foot of a mountain there was a long line of beach like a silver streak down across the brown foothills.

"Wouldn't it be nice," said George, "to go over there in the boat."

"Oh, no," said Conor. "I couldn't do that."

"Why not?" George asked. "Can't you handle it?"

"Yes," said Conor, "but my father would kill me."

"Well," said George, "he couldn't kill you until we got back, so what loss would be on you, as they say over here?"

This made them laugh.

"Aw, I couldn't, I couldn't," said Conor.

George saw he was weakening. If you say a thing twice it means you are not sure.

"Would it take long to go over there and back?" he asked.

"A few hours," said Conor.

"Who'd know then?" George asked.

"It's not that," said Conor.

"What is it?" George asked.

"It's just I wouldn't like taking it without telling my father," said Conor.

"Have you taken it out fishing before?" asked George.

"Oh, yes," said Conor," with some of the lads."

"Well, we're some of the lads," said George. "Let's go. We will be there and back before anyone is the wiser. Wouldn't you like to go to that beach by water, Edwin?"

Edwin's gaze was wistful.

"I'd like to very much," said Edwin.

"You'd have to row," said Conor. "Have you handled oars before?"

"My grandfather invented them," said George.

"All right," said Conor, yielding. "But I'm sure my father will kill me."

"We'll go to the funeral," said George. "Where are the oars?"

Conor laughed and walked back to where the oars were

stuffed between the rocks under a whitehorn bush. They were long, heavy oars with very narrow blades. There were holes near the handles to fit on the pegs in the thwarts.

They helped him with them.

"This is more like it," said George. "This is the first time this vacation has started to look up."

"I'll sit at the first two oars," said Conor. "George, you take the two behind me, and, Edwin, you can sit in the stern until we call on you to row. In with ye."

George got on the seat between the second pair of oars, Edwin sat in the stern, and Conor freed the rope holding the boat and was prepared to get in, when a small voice beside them said, "I tell Daddy."

This stopped them. They looked at Babo.

He was standing there with his finger in his mouth, very innocent.

"What'd he say?" George asked.

"He said he'll tell my father," said Conor.

"Betrayed," said George.

"We'll have to compromise," said Edwin.

"How?" asked Conor, frowning.

"Suppose, Babo," said Edwin, "that you came in here in the boat and sat with me. Then you wouldn't tell Daddy, would you?"

Babo smiled. He shook his head.

"See," said Edwin. "That's solved."

"But we'd have to take him with us," said Conor.

"You have to compromise," said Edwin.

"Throw him in," said George. "If we want to get rid of

him later, we have lovely deep water outside." He leered at Babo, but Babo wasn't upset.

"Oh," groaned Conor.

"Come on, Babo," said Edwin and reached for him, lifted him in, and tucked him between his knees. "Cast off, skipper," he said.

Conor hesitated for a moment, and then, shrugging his shoulders with resignation, freed the line, threw it in, and got in behind the oars.

They maneuvered the boat carefully out of the little harbor and into the wide water. Conor started to row, a sort of chopping stroke, describing an oval. They had fun for a few minutes as George got his oars all tangled up with Conor's, but he soon found the simple rhythm, and they went quite fast over the calm water.

Conor should have noticed that there wasn't a boat left on the waters of the bay, and that as they got farther out, the calm of the water was a very oily calm, a lurking calm.

There was a person on one of the headlands, waving his arms at them. He was shouting "Come back! Come back!" but they couldn't hear his words and waved cheerfully back at him.

There was a heavy, copper-colored mist covering the sky from the northeast, where the mountains were. It had already enveloped the mountains and blotted them out, and when they were about five hundreds yards out, heading for the faraway silver beach, the first ominous ripples started to disturb the waters of the bay.

chapter

3

People remarked afterward how swiftly the wind built up. It would be remembered and talked about for a good many years, until a worse one came.

Conor didn't notice it at first. After all, there was just the sound of the sudden small waves hitting against the side of the boat. It was enough to make him look around him, and when he did he was startled at what he saw. The wind was coming through a sort of funnel in the mountains, and a great buildup of water was coming directly toward them with the speed of an arrow. It was as if an enormous sea animal were speeding toward them a little under the surface and making white water with his back.

It was only then that he looked around the bay and noticed the complete absence of boats.

"George!" he shouted, dismayed to find that he had to

shout because the wind was whining all around them. "Pull your left oar! Pull your left oar! We will have to turn back."

He pulled on his own left oar. That brought them around slowly, so that the stern of the boat was pointed back toward the place where the wind was coming from. He was frightened when he saw the deep darkness of the cloud that was coming as if to swallow them, its blackness making the breaking waves seem all the whiter.

He pulled frantically again with his left oar. He thought they might be able to go back to the shore sideways to the waves. They could have if they had been normal waves, if they had been just the waves of a summer storm. But these waves were phenomenal.

It was as if they were caught in a maelstrom. Even if they had been grown men with mighty muscles they would never have been able to hold the boat sideways to the wind. Because it was so light and carrying no great weight, the currach was riding on top of the waves like a paper boat.

It was a terrifying experience. One moment they would be on top of the world, almost it seemed on a level with the mountains on their right, which were not yet blotted out, and the next moment they would be deep in a trough, looking up at a wave ten or twelve feet over their heads. If it had been a heavier boat they would have been engulfed, but this boat rose like a cork and dropped like a cork.

Conor knew the best thing to do would be to face the

boat into the wind and the weather and try to hold on, but this was impossible. His left arm felt as if it were paralyzed and he was forced to ease the strain on it. Immediately the boat turned its stern to the waves and ran before the weather.

"Hold, George! Hold!" he shouted.

They were high, high and then they were deep in the trough. He saw an enormous wave behind about to swallow them and he called, "Pull! Pull!" and pulled just when the wave seemed about to pour itself into them. It was a feeble effort, but with the little pull and the buoyancy of the boat it seemed to save them from disaster.

"Bail, Edwin! Bail!" he shouted.

It was Babo who reached behind them and pulled out the old blackened saucepan and handed it to him. They were practically sitting in water. It had all happened so fast that Edwin was bewildered. He had read the whole story on Conor's face as it happened. He had never known that the sea could be like this. You read stories about it, and of ships being destroyed by the fury of the gales, but you didn't believe the sea could have such power. He tucked Babo well in under him and started to bail out the water with the black saucepan. It seemed a ridiculous thing to do, but he knew it kept his mind on something and stopped his heart from jumping out of his mouth.

That was the way it went. Pull! Pull! Bail! Bail!

George kept his eyes on Conor's back. He took his cue

from the movement of Conor's shoulders. He tried to keep his oars high until he had to plunge them into the water as Conor did so, but it was a hard job, because when the wind wasn't tearing at them the water was. He was awed by the look of the sky behind them. Nobody who hadn't seen it could believe that it could change so fast.

Conor was thinking of himself standing on the high ground looking over the calm bay this morning and his stomach went cold as he thought of the map of it. In the direction they were being blown there must be at least a million rocks: big black ones, standing out of the water; big long flat ones lurking under the water; reefs of them here and there. The main channel of the bay was much farther out.

Conor thought, There is absolutely no way that we can be saved. There is no way at all in the world that we can be blown out of the bay without hitting one of the great rock beds. They were all jagged, like knife blades. He knew that they would cut the boat to bits in a few seconds and that they would cut their bodies to bits in the same way.

He thought, Why did I do this? I am responsible for the death of these nice boys. Their people will be crying for them forever, all because I was stupid and wanted to boast about the boat and show them how well I could handle it.

He saw Babo's face peering out at him from under Edwin's chest, and he groaned. The little fellow would be gone. He knew how everyone at home would be desolate over him, he was so loved.

"I'm sorry! I'm sorry!" Conor shouted.

"What? What?" Edwin asked.

"Pull! Pull!" shouted Conor as he saw the great wave behind him, and they inched away from the full force of its fall.

He heard the new noise behind him, and his stomach tightened. It was a new sound over the fury of all the other sounds. He knew it was the great waves scouring the black rocks.

He waited, terror-stricken, saying nothing, just waiting, and out of the corner of his eye he saw it as they were swept past, like an acre of white pudding it was reaching for them, and then it was behind them and Conor had to bend down his head and close his eyes with the relief.

But George was calling "Conor! Conor!" and he raised his head and saw a new wave behind them as tall as a cliff, ready to fall on them, so he straightened up and gripped his oars and pulled, and it barely missed them.

He didn't know how long the storm lasted. He was never able to know or guess how long. The rain came on top of them, a deluge, not falling straight down but coming at them from behind, like long silver lances, blinding them, closing all around them so that they had to guess at the terrors beyond the short radius of their vision. At least, Conor thought, we will never know when we hit.

They didn't hit. Only Conor knew how near they came to it at least ten times. One time he saw only a yard of distance separating them from total destruction. And the rain was cold and numbed their senses. This was good, he thought.

For two seconds the mist lifted and on his left he saw, over his shoulder, the outline of the land. One glimpse of it was all he got, but he knew it. It was the last island in the bay. Beyond that there was nothing but three thousand miles of water to America.

"Right! Right! Right, George!" Conor shouted, hoping he would hear him. "Pull right."

It was a slim chance, but he knew that the island was standing in the path of the great gale. A long headland of it would be daring the northeast wind, and behind this headland there might be a great sheltered calm.

"Right! Right! Right!" he kept shouting as he pulled. He let his left oar trail. It was immediately clamped against the side of the boat as if it had been done with springs. George did the same. Conor put his two hands on the right oar and strained and pulled until he thought he would burst all the veins in his body. He heard George grunting and knew he was doing the same.

He couldn't tell if it would do any good. He couldn't tell, looking behind, if they were winning their way a little toward the left. But he kept straining and pulling, and then he saw the rocks as they were swept past them, rocks that weren't single, but attached to the rising land.

"Right! Right!" he kept shouting. The boat seemed to

be taken now and swept doubly fast, like a ball in flight that is sent faster with an added blow.

He couldn't believe it when he felt the strain lessening on his arm. He looked behind them. He saw the headland that made the little bay. They were in swirling water. But there were no giant waves. Conor knew that if they drifted they would soon be blown out among them again.

"Two oars, George!" he shouted. "Pull two! Pull two!"

He pulled himself. He felt George taking up the rhythm. It wasn't easy. The little vicious, choppy waves were only poor relations of the ones outside, but they were related. But after what they had come through, they seemed like nothing at all, nothing at all, and the most beautiful sound they were ever to hear in their lives was the bottom of the boat grating on pebbles and settling into sand.

Conor looked at Edwin. Edwin looked at Conor. Conor felt the hand of George hitting his shoulder and he dropped his head on his knees.

He was trembling all over. He wondered if it was a dream and he would hear his mother coming and saying, "Conor! Conor! Get up. It's time to go to school."

chapter
4

They pulled the boat far up on the beach, free from the waves. George pounded his feet on the sand.

"Look," he said. "It's real. I thought we'd never feel it. Where are we, Conor?"

"We were lucky," said Conor. "This is the last island in the bay. It is called Ox Island." He wondered why he felt disturbed by the sound of the name. "We'd better go up and look around. Come on, Babo." He bent down so that Babo could get up on his back. He felt an affection for Babo, now that they were all safe when they shouldn't be. Babo put his arms around his neck and curled his legs around his waist.

Conor started to climb the rocks that shut them in. He felt his wet clothes. They were all of them wet. The rain had stopped, he noticed, but the wind was still high. They didn't feel it on the sheltered beach but once they climbed higher and got onto the smooth, grassy ground on top, he had to pause and lean into the wind. When they got to the height and looked back at the bay he had to close his eyes to slits in order to see against the force of the wind and the driving spray.

"Boy!" said George as they looked.

"How did we come through that?" Edwin asked.

"I don't know," said Conor. "I truly don't know."

They couldn't see far as it was closed in on all sides, but what they could see was ripped and tortured with the wind and the rocks. Wherever the rocks were the water was thrown high, high into the sky, a white mass that was being beheaded by the slicing wind. All the same, Conor didn't think the same force was in the wind.

"It won't last long," he told them. "Then we can go home."

"Let's look around the island while we are waiting," said George.

"There's not much to see," said Conor. "It's just an old island."

"Hey, look," said Edwin. "There's a boat. It's a big one."

He was pointing to his right.

It was a big white cabin cruiser riding at anchor inside the headland, shut off by a spur from where they had landed. There was another beach in from it and an inflated yellow dinghy was resting on the sand.

"It is," said Conor. "It is a boat. Now we are safe. They'll bring us home when the wind dies."

"Well, let's go down and see them," said George.

"Maybe they'll have something to eat. Boy, we're lucky."

He ran ahead of them. There was a path down to the beach. Conor knew that sometimes men brought sheep from the mainland to graze the island, and they had crude landing places here and there that might be sheltered from any of the winds that were blowing.

George got there first, and he cupped his mouth with his hands and called, "Hi, there! Hi, there!"

Edwin said, "It's no use calling them. They must be on the island when the dinghy is pulled up on the beach."

"Well, let's track them down," said George. "They can't be far away. It's not an awful big island. Come on." He ran away from them. He had long legs. Edwin set off after him. Conor brought up the rear. Babo was nice and fat, so he was heavy.

"Hungry," said Babo in Conor's ear.

"All right," said Conor. "Don't worry. We'll get you something to eat soon. Don't worry."

The island was like a saucer. Here on their left was a big head of solid rock with a coat of green grass on the west side. It was like a person's head gazing down at the saucer below. This was about twenty acres around. It held lots of grass and yellowing bracken and low thorn bushes. Not a tree, because no tree could live out here in the path of the almost perpetual winds. There were old ruins in the center of the saucer. A thousand years before, there had been monks living on this island. They had built a church, but none of it remained now except some ruins—ivy-covered stones and part of a pointed window.

George was shouting again, "Hi, there! Hi, there!" but his shouting was being lost in the wind.

Conor knew there was a beehive cell on the other side of the ruins, just where the land rose again to the great cliff that was now taking a battering from the storm. He wondered if the people would be sheltering in the cell.

They passed the ruins and then came into a big green field which was cropped closely by the sheep. The cell was right in the middle of this field, about twenty or thirty yards from the second head that rose to look into the bay, and suddenly from this head two people came to meet him.

George ran toward them, saying, "Hi there, are we glad to see you!" Edwin was following him, smiling, and suddenly Conor stood stock still, because he saw that they were the two he had seen in the cruiser. The man was a huge fat man wearing a sailor's jacket and a yachting cap. The woman was tall and thin, dressed in heavy tweed clothes. Even from there he could see her beak of a nose and her long, bony wrists, and suddenly he remembered her eyes and how she had looked at him, and now she raised her eyes and looked at him again, and suddenly pointed a finger at him.

"There he is, Captain," she said in a shrill voice. "There he is! That's the one! Grab him! Don't let him get away!"

He saw the astonishment on the captain's face.

"Go on," she was screaming, "don't let him get away!"

He saw the captain moving toward him, walking and then beginning to trot, so he turned and ran.

George said, "What's going on here? Listen, leave him alone."

That was all Conor heard, because he was running as hard as he could toward the edge of the saucer. He knew if he got over the edge that he could play tag with them for hours among the rocks of the shore.

Babo was a burden to him. He could run twice as fast if he hadn't had him on his back.

"Come back! Come back!" he heard the captain calling in a deep voice. "Nobody will hurt you."

Conor wasn't so sure. He remembered the look in the woman's eyes and he wasn't taking any chances. His heart pounding, he ran until he reached the edge, turned on his stomach there, and let himself down to the rocks. He went to the right, wondering how Babo had stayed on his back in the flight. He crouched behind a big rock, his eyes glued to the top, eased Babo from his back, and said to him, "Stay quiet now! Stay quiet!" Babo clutched his hand.

The captain had turned back halfway.

"Agnes," he said, "this is ridiculous. There are other boys with him. What can you do?"

"Find out what he saw!" she said. "Find out what he saw!"

She turned now to George and Edwin, who had edged away from them, wondering what was up, but ready to flee.

"What did he tell you?" she called. "What did that boy tell you?"

"Nothing," George shouted. "We were caught in the

storm. We are lucky to be alive. All he told us was that this is Ox Island."

"You see!" she said to the captain. "He told them. They know! He saw the map. He'll talk. They'll talk."

"They know nothing much," the captain said. "Agnes, don't become unbalanced over this thing."

"Unbalanced!" she said. "It took me fourteen years, fourteen years to find it. You saw it yourself. You know this is the place. Do you think that I am going to be frustrated now!" She turned then toward the two boys and called to them imperiously, "Come here, you two!"

The wind was blowing her cropped white hair. George and Edwin looked at her, then they looked at one another, and then they ran toward the spot where Conor had disappeared over the edge.

"Come back! Come back!" she called after them, but they didn't stop.

She looked after them. There were sparks coming out of her eyes. She clenched her hands.

"After all those years! All those years! To be frustrated by a lot of stupid boys. How did they get here?"

"They must have been in a boat and got blown here in the storm," said the captain.

"Why didn't the storm kill them?" she asked. "How could they have weathered a storm like that? Let's go and see what kind of a boat they came in."

"Agnes, what are you going to do?" he asked.

"Do?" she said. "Why, nothing, Captain. We are just going to do nothing. Come on!"

She rode off toward the other head.

The captain looked after her thoughtfully. The boys looked pale and frightened to him, and possibly hungry. His normal inclination would be toward talking to them, feeding them. If he was his own man. But then, he wasn't. He would always do what she wanted. That was his weakness. And he too was excited at the thought that they were so near to success. Still, it was a pity the boys had come like this.

The wind was dying off, he noticed as he followed after her. The white mist was being pierced now and again by a shaft of afternoon sunlight.

"Conor! Conor!" Edwin was calling softly.

Conor didn't answer until he was sure it was Edwin. Then he showed himself.

"Hello," he said sheepishly.

"Wow, Conor," said George. "You have the most peculiar friends."

"They are no friends of mine," said Conor. "That old lady frightens the daylights out of me."

"Where did you meet them before?" Edwin asked.

Conor told them.

"But what did you see?" asked Edwin.

"Nothing," said Conor. "Nothing at all. I can't remember a thing I saw."

"Did you hear what they said?" George asked.

"Sort of," said Conor. "It was all mixed up. I wasn't listening properly."

"We'll have to see what they are up to," said George. "Come on!" He climbed back up the rocks and peeped into the saucer. "They're going back," he said. "Come on, we'll have to see what they are up to."

He climbed up. They followed him, Conor swinging Babo on his back again.

When they got up there was no sign of them.

"They are going back to the boat, I think," said George. "We'll keep close on their tails, but be ready to run."

They followed very cautiously, with George going ahead and making signals with his hand.

Finally, they got to a place where they could look down and see what was happening. Conor could feel warmth from the sun on his wet clothes. At least, he thought, we can be thankful for that and that the storm is dying. All the same it would be very dark before the sea was calm enough for them to row home.

They weren't destined to row home, as they soon saw.

The woman was on the cruiser and the captain was rowing away from it. They wondered why, and when they saw why they were astounded.

The captain came back again, pulling *their* boat after him toward the cruiser.

"Look what he's doing," said George. "He's taking our boat!"

They were so astonished that they couldn't answer him.

They watched him reach the cruiser. They saw them

talking. The captain was objecting, they could see, but he shrugged his shoulders and then took the long knife she handed down to him. He got into the currach and put the oars of it under the thwarts, tied them and threw a block of iron ballast into the stern. Then he bent down and slashed, slashed with the knife. He left the currach then, got into the dinghy, from there into the cruiser, and then he hauled the dinghy aboard the cruiser. He was a strong man.

There was the currach going down. It went very fast. He had slashed the canvas all over. They saw the water covering it in, gurgling, and then it was gone and there was the black saucepan floating on the water. That was all.

George was standing up, shouting, "Here, you can't do that! You can't do that!"

They paid no attention to him.

Conor was horrified. He thought of how carefully his father had made the currach, and now it was at the bottom of the sea. What would he say to Conor for the loss of his boat?

The engine started up on the cruiser, the captain hauled the anchor, the boat reversed, turned, and then in a wide sweep headed out into the rough water back into the bay. The waves tossed it, but it was a heavy boat and was soon gone from their sight.

Conor had scrambled down toward the beach.

The backlash of the water outside was driving the saucepan in toward the shore.

He stood there waiting for it, hoping that it wouldn't be swamped before it reached him. It was the only thing left.

He reached for it and got it.

The others were standing behind him.

"Do you fellows know that we are marooned?" Edwin asked.

"Maybe we're dreaming," said George.

"That was what I hoped too," said Conor.

"I'm hungry," said Babo.

The three of them looked at him.

"I wish you hadn't said that, Babo," said George. "I'm hungry too."

"That's good," said Edwin, "because we have nothing to eat. When did we eat last, George?"

"Breakfast," said George. "If I'd only known."

"We might be able to get some blackberries," said Conor.

"Anything," said George. "Where are they?"

Conor walked ahead of them, They were silent now. It was only beginning to dawn on them that they were in trouble. Too much had happened to them in a few hours. It was hard to take it all in.

There were blackberries. A lot of them were not good because it was late August and their time was over, but by careful collecting they managed to get the saucepan about half filled, and then they divided the berries into four portions, Conor noticing that Babo's portion seemed to be bigger than the others. They ate the berries slowly and they tasted quite nice, but they were no substitute for a six-course dinner, as George pointed out.

They couldn't believe it. The sun nearly dried their clothes, but they stood on the headland for hours, watching to see if a boat would come for them. It didn't come. When the moon rose to look at them, they turned back into the field of the cell. It was a beehive-shaped cell, made by men a thousand years ago, but it was sound and dry and they went in there when Conor had swept out the sheep droppings with a makeshift bracken broom. They got close together with Babo in the middle of them, and because they were boys they slept.

Edwin had said, "In the morning. We'll sort it all out in the morning."

chapter

5

Conor heard the funny chopping sound, far off, some-
what like the noise of a mowing machine or a tractor.

He sat up. His body was stiff. He felt cold. It took him
a little while to realize where he was. Then his heart
started sinking as the cold knowledge dawned on him.
He thought he might have been dreaming about the
noise. He listened. He could still hear it.

He got carefully to his feet. Babo was sleeping on his
back. Edwin had an arm about his body.

He went through the opening and stood outside.
There was a sort of white fog over everything, low lying
because he could see the head rising over it. He ran
toward the south end of the island, running fast, glad to
feel the blood warming in his body.

When he came to the bay where the cruiser had rested,
he climbed a rock and looked around him.

The sea was covered with the white mist, in patches. It was calm. Over his head he could see patches of blue sky, and now and again he felt the warmth of the hidden sun on his body. He wished he were a giant so that he could blow away the white mist.

He even pursed his lips, inflated his chest, and blew at it, and then he had to laugh because it seemed that for a moment he had blown it all away. The veils parted between himself and the faraway mainland, and it was then he saw the helicopter. It was about halfway between himself and the mainland, flying low when it came to a small island and circling.

His heart leapt with hope. He turned and ran back again toward the cell, jumping over the stones and the clumps of gorse that were in his way.

He shouted in the opening, "Come on! Come on! They are looking for us. Hey! Hey! They are looking for us!" He didn't wait for them. He saw that his shouts had brought them awake. He ran back to his rock again, thinking, now it will be all right. I won't feel so much to blame. When they see us and take us out of here I will be able to laugh at all that has happened to us.

He soon felt them beside him.

"Where? Where?" George was asking.

"Look! Look!" said Conor, pointing.

"I see it," said George. "Oh, you beautiful mechanical dragonfly!"

"Over here! Over here!" Edwin shouted at it, waving his arms.

They were silent then for a while, watching it. It was working very methodically, but it wasn't getting any nearer to them. It was working the small islands and the rocks and moving in to the far shore, and soon they could hardly see it; it was just like a black fly.

"Maybe when he has done the shore he will come out here," said Conor. "He'll have to, won't he?"

Edwin sat down on the rock.

"Your friends went in last night," he said. "They would have asked them, 'Did you see any sign of four boys and a boat?' And what would they say?"

"Oh, oh," said George. "I see what you mean. They would say, 'Well, we were out on this Ox Island all during the storm, and we saw no sign of boys or boat.' Is that what you mean?"

"That's it," said Edwin.

"So they would say, 'Well, if they are not on Ox Island that's one place we don't have to look.'"

"Right," said Edwin.

"But they wouldn't do a thing like that," said Conor.

The two boys looked at him silently.

"I don't think anyone would do a thing like that," he said lamely then, thinking of the woman's eyes.

"What were they talking about, Conor?" Edwin asked. "Think. It depends on the importance of it. It must be big or they wouldn't have left us marooned here to starve to death or something."

"I wasn't really listening," said Conor. He squeezed his forehead with his fingers. "It was something about the tale of Cathbadh, and about the great stone, and the Island of the Great Yellow Ox, and I think she said that this had to be the one because it was the island of the two heads. That's all. I can't remember. It was all senseless.

"But they wouldn't leave us here like this, would they?" he went on. "Who would do a thing like that?"

"They have done it," said George. "We have to face it."

"But our people will think that we are all dead," said Conor.

They looked at one another and then looked away.

They could barely see the helicopter at all now. They thought of their families and how they would feel.

"I'm hungry," said the voice of Babo, beside them.

They looked at him. His hands were behind his back. He looked as if he was going to cry.

"Go down on the stones," said Conor, "and get yourself some bairneacs."

Babo thought this over and then obeyed. He climbed down the rocks to the seaweed-covered shore below them.

"What's bairneacs?" George asked.

"I don't know. Just bairneacs," said Conor.

They watched the little fellow taking a stone in his pudgy fist and hitting at the thing on the rock.

"Oh, you mean limpets," said Edwin. "Can you eat them?"

"Barnacles, you mean," said George. "What are they like?"

"They are all right," said Conor.

Babo had knocked one off the rock. Now they saw him free it from the shell with his fingers, scoop away the bottom brown part and start to eat the rest.

"It looks awful," said Edwin.

"Unless my mom sees my dead body," said George, "she won't believe that I'm dead. I bet you. My mom will end up having the whole American fleet over here looking for us. I bet you."

"But they will think that we were just all wiped out in the storm," said Edwin.

"No," said Conor suddenly. "They shouldn't have sunk the boat. My father won't believe it unless he can find a piece of the boat, even a small piece, oars or something. They should have let the boat drift in and be smashed up, then he might have believed."

They looked at one another. They felt a bit more cheerful.

"I don't think my father would go home without me without more evidence either," said Edwin.

"So these people can't keep us hidden forever," said Conor. "Won't they be in great trouble with the police when we tell all about them?"

They looked at one another again.

"If they let us tell all about them," said George.

They felt dismayed again.

Edwin rose to his feet.

"Look," he said, "we'll have to get organized. Empty your pockets. Let's see what we have." He knelt down and started to turn out his own. They followed his example.

They leaned down then and looked at the collection.

It wasn't much. Two handkerchiefs, not very clean, a multicolored glass marble, a golf ball, a small silver-colored pocket knife, a piece of pink chalk, a short length of string and one fish hook stuck in a piece of cardboard, and one mint candy wrapped in green paper.

"Not much there," said Edwin. "The knife and the fish hook." He took the mint. He stood up.

"Here, Babo," he said. "Look what we found. Here's a treat for you." He threw it. It fell near him. Babo found it and slowly peeled off the paper and put the candy in his mouth. Their own mouths started to water at the sight.

"The next thing we do," said Edwin, "is to scour the shore while the tide is out. We'll divide it into three parts. We'll search, and everything we find we'll bring back to the cell. Right?"

"Wood," said Conor. "If we had driftwood we might be able to light a fire and cook something."

"What?" George asked. "Babo? There would be a nice succulent dish."

They laughed.

"It's *doing* something that's important," said Edwin. "Let's go."

They were over an hour coming and going. The only good thing about it was that it was turning into a fine sunny day, and the sun was warm on their bodies.

As he searched the shore Conor was very apprehensive. He thought of the parents of George and Edwin and how they must be feeling since yesterday, all the searching of the shore when they heard. Because they had been seen. Conor remembered the person waving from the shore and shouting, he now knew, "Come back! Come back!" He would know and would have told. Boats would be out all over the bay. They would search this island too if they hadn't been told that there was no use searching.

He thought it was a good omen when he found the bottom of the green glass bottle. It was good and thick.

He shouted, "I got it! I got it!"

He had his part of the shore searched, so he gathered all that he had and headed back toward the cell.

He didn't have a lot.

Driftwood was scarce on this shore because it was so far out in the ocean. He had some, an armful, made up of pieces of flat wood, bits of boxes that had come adrift from the fishing boats, bits of tree timber that had drifted out from the mainland, but it was all well washed and scoured and there would be little firepower in it. Still, he knew that if they could get a fire to light they would be able to eat something, however small it might be.

The others weren't back. He went to the old wall of the monastery and cleared a space there where the wall angled. It would provide a little shelter and a little draft. He went to the bracken and took off a few of the fronds that were turning brown. He also got a few strips of the dead blackberry briars, and he tore one of the handkerchiefs into linen shreds. Then he made a small pile of these things and got down on his belly, and catching the rays of the sun in the bottom of the broken bottle he reflected them onto his little heap.

He directed the beam at the bracken and the linen threads.

He watched it closely. He didn't turn his head when he felt the others kneeling beside him. He just watched the beam and, as it began to scorch, he held his breath. When a small, burnt hole began to appear in it, he gently blew at it with his mouth, and dropped a few tiny pieces of the bracken on the hole. They began to smoke, and he fed the smoke with more, and that smoked, and suddenly the little pile burst into a tiny flame, so he heaped pieces of the briars around this and they took fire, and then the three of them started tearing tiny strips of wood from the timber, and burned them around this flame, and in ten minutes they saw the fire ready to blaze.

"Keep it fed now, Edwin," said Conor. "We'll get the saucepan, and we'll go and get cockles and mussels if we can, and we'll cook a potful of them."

"Boy! Seafood!" said George. "Let's go."

It wasn't easy. There was only one small beach of sand where they could get cockles. Conor walked on this, looking for the telltale pinholes the cockles make, and then bending to scoop them before they burrowed in the sand. The mussels were easier. There were many of them clustered on the rocks on the east side of the island.

The trouble then was that the saucepan was small and mussels are big. They boiled one lot of them, and they were so hungry by the time they had opened to disclose their yellow contents that their hands were trembling.

Babo alone would have eaten all they cooked, so they had to ration him. By the time they had cooked three saucepansful and eaten them they were still hungry, and their stock of firewood was dwindling alarmingly.

"If only we could get one big fish, one big fish," said George. "I'd eat him raw."

"It's a pity my father's fishing lines are in the bottom of the boat," said Conor, "or we could have caught fish with them."

"What did you say?" George asked.

"You remember the lines in the currach," said Conor. "There were two of them with lead weights."

"That's what I thought you said," said George, and without another word he got up and ran.

"Hey, where are you going, George?" Edwin asked.

He didn't answer them.

"He must be going after the fishing lines," said Conor. They looked at each another.

"There's no way," said Edwin.

"They are at the bottom of the sea," said Conor.

"But George is half fish," said Edwin, rising.

"Let's go," said Conor cheerfully and ran after George.

Edwin was about to run when he saw Babo's face.

He bent his back.

"Up," he said to him, and when he felt the soft arms around his neck, he followed after the running boys.

chapter

6

By the time they reached the small bay, George had already thrown off his clothes and was swimming with a swift crawl to the spot where their boat had been slashed and sunk.

Conor ran out along the black rock forming one side of the bay and stood where he thought the cruiser had anchored. When George, who was dog-paddling around trying to get his bearings, saw him pointing, he took a deep breath and dived.

They watched tensely. All that remained of him was the swirl on the water.

"Where's George gone?" Babo asked.

"He's diving," said Edwin.

"Why?" asked Babo.

"He's trying to get down to the boat to get the fishing lines," said Edwin.

"Why is the boat down there?" Babo asked.

Why, Edwin thought, Babo is hardly more than a baby. He doesn't understand what this is all about. He sat down beside him on the rock and put his arms around him.

"It got sunk," he said. How could he explain why?

"The storm," said Babo.

"That's right," said Edwin, thinking what cruel people those two were to leave a child like this, and his mother crying for him. He wondered what motive they had that could be powerful enough to make them do such a thing.

George came from below and took a great gulp of air. He shook his head, breathed heavily again, and dived.

"Why do we want fishing lines?" Babo asked.

"We want to try and catch fish," said Edwin. "We have nothing else to eat."

"I'm hungry," said Babo. "I'd like bread and jam."

"He'll drive you mad asking questions," said Conor.

"He has a perfect right to ask questions," said Edwin.

"He's getting around you well," said Conor, laughing.

"I'd love a lick of bread and jam myself," said Edwin, the smell of fresh bread momentarily in his nostrils.

"I want to go home," said Babo.

"We'll go home when we get a boat," said Edwin.

"When will we get a boat?" asked Babo.

"I don't know when, but we'll get one," said Edwin.

Then George was up again.

"I found it!" he shouted.

This cry brought them to their feet.

"Great man, George!" Conor shouted at him.

"It's deep," George shouted. "I don't know if I can get it."

He took several deep breaths again and dived.

Conor knew the kind of ground it was. It was a rocky bottom and there would be long weed waving from the rocks. He hoped that George wouldn't be caught in the weeds. He had an image of him down there, his long white body swimming in and out of the weeds. He hoped nothing would happen to him, not on account of the fishing lines, but because he was George.

They waited tensely now. He seemed to be under for ages.

"How long can he stay down without breathing?" Conor asked.

"Now who's asking questions?" Edwin jeered.

"Ah, how long?" Conor pleaded.

"About three minutes," said Edwin.

"He seems to be gone longer than that," said Conor.

"He isn't," said Edwin.

The first thing that came out of the water was a hand holding a fishing frame. They cheered, laughing, and then George's smiling face came out and he raised the other hand and there was a frame in that too. He turned on his back and kicked his way swiftly toward them. They went down to him and Conor took the fishing frames from him. He looked at them to see if they were all right. They were. The fishing line was good and there were two hooks at the end of each and a lead weight.

George was lying on his back, half in and half out of the water. He was breathing heavily.

"What is it like, George?" Conor asked, bending down to him.

"Deep, man," said George. "The boat is wedged between two big rocks. I tried to heave at it, but it wouldn't budge. We'd never get it up without some heavy tackle."

"Well, that's that then," said Edwin.

"Let's go and try for fish now," said Conor.

"I'd nearly eat one raw, if we could get it," said George. "Have you ever eaten raw fish, Edwin?"

"Yes," said Edwin, "but sort of pickled, and only little bits."

"Think of that dinner in the hotel," said George. "Shrimp cocktail, soup, smoked salmon, steak and mushrooms, baked alaska. Oh, boy!"

"Please, George," said Edwin in a pained voice. They laughed at him.

Conor wondered why they were laughing. They hadn't much to laugh about. The fact that they had lines didn't mean that they automatically had fish. Fish were funny. You didn't get them when you expected them and when you didn't you did. Moody, his father said, like women. He thought of his father and his father's boat slashed at the bottom of the sea.

"Let's go and fish," he said, to blot out his thoughts. He set off toward the westerly part of the island, carrying the frames. He knew the welter of big rocks

over there was a good place for fishing. He had seen the
boats working around there when he was out with his
father.

Edwin and Babo waited for George. He rubbed the
wet off his body with his hands before he dressed
himself.

"Were you afraid down there, George?" Edwin asked.

"No," said George, "but I was cold. At home when we
go diving the water is warm. When you go deep out here
it's like ice."

"Did you see people?" Babo asked.

George laughed.

"No, Babo," he said. "They haven't gotten down there
yet. That's the nice thing about the deep, that there are
no people."

George was soon dressed and they set out to follow
Conor.

He was sitting on a rock, paring the lead weight with
the small knife.

"It's too heavy," he told them. "It would sink too fast.
It's meant to travel behind a moving boat and that keeps
it off the bottom."

It was a tough job paring it with the little knife. He
was afraid he would break the knife. Now and again he
would sharpen the small edge of it on a stone. The
weight was an elongated one with eyes at both ends
where the lines were tied to it. The lead came off in silver
slivers.

"The next time I am going to be marooned," said

George, "I am going to make sure that I have a jackknife in my pocket, and a two-way radio and dozens and dozens of twenty-four-hour rations."

"And a sleeping bag," said Edwin, "and soap and towels and boxes of matches."

They were lying on the rocks. The sun was very warm. The sea was calm, just heaving now and again near the island.

"And a small electric generator," continued George, "and one of those yellow rubber boats that inflate themselves."

"Wouldn't that be funny?" Edwin asked. "When you were on vacation, every time you went out to play you would have to have all those things with you."

"Only," said George, "if you knew you were going to meet fellows like Conor, who would take you out in a boat in a storm and get you wrecked on an island, and have first-class friends with fire coming out of their eyes at the sight of you."

"Ah, listen, fellas," said Conor.

"Shh," said Edwin to George, nodding at Babo.

George turned to him and rubbed his hair.

"Aren't you having fun, Babo?" he asked. "Isn't this a great adventure?"

"I want to go home," said Babo.

"So you will, old Babo, any day now. You just wait."

"I'm ready to try this one now," said Conor. He swung the end of the line and the weight. It whistled.

"I can bait it over there," he said.

He headed out toward a finger of rocks that pushed

into the sea. He had to clamber up them, sliding off sometimes, and getting wet to the waist in the pools. The last rock he could reach was broad and jagged, but it gave him a firm footing. About ten yards from this there was another cluster of big rocks, making a channel. He dug mussels from a cluster, opened a few of them, and put their contents firmly on the two hooks.

Then he swung the line, having freed most of it from the frame, and put the rest of the line and the frame under his foot, and it sailed out toward the far rocks and plopped into the water.

He allowed for the weight to sink the bait a certain depth and then he started taking it in with his fingers slowly, waiting to feel the tug of the fish. He waited in vain that time. He gathered in the line and swung it and let it sail away again in a slightly different direction.

"I think he's wasting his time," said George. "I never saw fish being caught that way."

"Maybe there's no fish down there," said Edwin.

"Yow!" Conor roared, and they ran toward him, climbing and scrambling and calling "Hold him, Conor! Hold him!" and feeling sorry for their lack of faith in him.

He was drawing in the line. They could see it straining, being pulled left and right.

"It's a biggish fellow," said Conor.

"Don't lose him," said George.

They watched the flash of the fish in the water, sort of white and yellow.

"It's a pollock," said Conor. "It's a big one."

"Can you eat it?" George asked. "As if I wouldn't eat shark even."

"Chicken," said Conor. "It's like boiled chicken. Here!" And he lifted the line and the fish flopped around in front of them on the rock in a pool. George fell on it.

"I'm not going to lose my chow," he said. He held the fish down with his hands, and pulled at the head of it until its spine broke and it lay still. He took the hook from its jaw and held it up. "Look," he said. "It's nearly a dinner for four." The fish was about three pounds in weight. "Suppose I get the other line, Conor, and we both get at it, we'll have enough for tomorrow too."

The word "tomorrow" seemed to rest on a silence as they looked at one another. They didn't want to be here tomorrow.

Edwin said, "You two keep fishing and Babo and I will go and collect some more firewood. We'll have to light a fire again while the sun is high. Here, how do we light a fire if there is no sun?"

They looked at one another.

"Unless we could find flint stone," said George.

"We won't be able to let the fire out," said Conor. "We'll have to keep feeding it little pieces to keep a spark in it."

"That means somebody has to be up all night," said George.

"We haven't much firewood," said Edwin. "If we had enough, we could light an enormous fire when it gets dark and people on the mainland would see it."

"We haven't enough," said Conor. "I doubt there is enough on the island. It's better to cook with it than that. And besides, on hot days like this mists come up at night and nobody could see the fire anyhow."

"Come on, Babo," said Edwin resignedly, "let's go and collect firewood." He called this back at the little fellow, who had not followed them. He scrambled back to him and took his hand and set off along the shore. George came to where the other frame was and, imitating Conor, started to pare the weight, while Conor swung the line and sent it soaring out.

At least, he thought, we have something substantial to eat. And that's a consolation. If they expected us to die of starvation they are mistaken. We'll show them!

chapter
7

Conor woke up feeling very cold. He wondered why. He was hugging himself with his arms. The sky was blue over his head with white fleecy clouds vanishing under the touch of the sun.

Then he turned his head and saw the ashes of the fire beside him. Oh, no, he thought, I have done something foolish again.

The fire seemed to be cold. He had fallen asleep when he was supposed to keep it alight.

He turned and felt it gingerly with his fingers. It was warm, but it wasn't hot. Then he poked around a little with a stick and saw an ember that wasn't quite dead. He separated this and blew on it gently. It glowed a little, so he kept after it, and when it was red he started to feed it, holding his breath, then blowing out at it.

He saved it. He was very glad. They had no idea of time. But last night they had divided the sky into segments, and as the moon, which was full, traveled the sky, they said, That's George part and that's Edwin's part, and the last part belongs to Conor.

And Conor had fallen asleep and nearly betrayed them, so he was overjoyed when the fire started to light again for him. There was very little wood left, so he was sparing with it. Today, he thought, we will have to gather the dried droppings of the sheep, since Edwin remembered Arabs lighting fires in the desert with camel dung. Maybe too, he thought, if they dried seaweed in the sun there would be some sort of heat from it.

The sun was high in the sky, he saw, so it must be late.

He got the four flat stones they used for plates. They had used them and washed them. He placed them on the ground, and then he got the saucepan, lifted the stone that acted as a lid, and doled out the boiled fish on the plates. It looked all right. There was a substantial helping for each of them, and they would be able to boil more of the fish today.

He bent at the opening to the cell and looked at the others.

They were lying on a bed of bracken. They had gathered a lot of the bracken, and it made a difference. It tickled a bit where it rubbed against the skin, but it was softer than the ground.

Babo was sleeping between the other two. He had one hand up at his cheek. He looked very young. Conor thought, He's not a bad little fellow at all. He doesn't keep crying all the time for his mommy.

"Wake up! Wake up!" he called. "The breakfast is ready! Hey! Hey! Wake up! Wake up!"

He watched them.

He knew the way they would feel. Where am I? Then, seeing the rough roof of the cell built with overlapping stones, they would think, What am I doing here? I should be in a nice soft bed and hearing the voice of my mother.

And it's my fault, he thought. Why did I do it?

"I'll have my breakfast in bed this morning, my good man," said Edwin. He was smiling, his hands under his head.

"Yeah," said George, "me too. Run my bath, bud."

Conor laughed and withdrew.

They soon followed him, stretching and yawning. They came and sat down in front of their plates. Babo started to eat immediately.

"What!" said George. "Fish again!"

"I'm beginning to feel like a fish," said Edwin.

"You smell like a fish," said George.

"It's fish or nothing," said Conor.

They were hungry and they ate, and they were almost finished when they heard the faraway throb of the boat engine.

"Listen," said Conor. They heard it then. It seemed to be approaching them. "No, don't run," said Conor as they rose to their feet. "You know, it might be those two. We want to think."

They thought it over. They agreed, and then, crouching, they ran toward the head that looked back into the bay.

They approached the edge of it on their bellies and looked out. They could see the white cruiser about a mile away, making toward the island. They drew back and leaned on their elbows.

"Now what do we do?" Conor asked.

"They won't expect us to be looking fit," said Edwin. "We will be lying in the cell when they come."

"We have to clear away everything," said George. "We hide the lines, traces of the fish, and the fire."

"Oh, no!" said Conor.

"We have to," said George. "We look very weak, no food, they get careless, and we may have a chance to steal the boat."

"Good tactics," said Edwin.

"And we hide Babo," said Conor. "I don't want them to find Babo."

"How will you hide him?" George asked.

"I'll find somewhere," said Conor with determination.

"Let's go fast," said George.

They did all those things. They threw a large flat rock over the fire. It covered even the burned bits of the grass. You wouldn't think there had been a fire.

Conor said to Babo, "Those two people are coming back, Babo."

"Are they bad peoples?" Babo asked.

"We don't like them," said Conor.

"I don't like them," said Babo, shaking his head.

"So we will hide you," said Conor. "Come on!"

They went to the shore where Conor had run the other day.

They quickly found a hiding place, two big rocks resting together and forming a little cavern. Babo easily fit in there. They put a few stones around the bottom and draped seaweed over the opening.

"You won't come out until we call you, Babo?" Conor asked anxiously.

"No," Babo promised. "I play jackstones." There were small stones between his legs. He took up a handful of them.

"Remember," said Conor. "Don't come out until we call you."

Babo was intent on his jackstones and didn't answer.

Going back, they came to a big stone that was a favorite resting place for the gulls. It was white and black with their accumulated droppings.

"We look too healthy," said George. "Here, rub a bit of this white stuff on your cheeks."

"Don't be silly," said Edwin.

"I'm not," said George. "My mom used to be an actress. I saw them. Did you ever see your mother with the white stuff on her face, the cream stuff? Looks like death."

He had rubbed some on his cheeks. He made a long face. They could see the red of his eyelids. He looked ghastly. They laughed. They rubbed it on their own faces and then, still crouching, they ran to the cell. They checked around it. No signs of fishbones, or the sauce-

60

pan. They went into the cell and sat in the gloomy interior with their backs to the wall, their hands listlessly on the ground, palms upturned.

They waited.

As they came near the island, looking up at the head, Lady Agnes said to the captain, "Look, you can even see it from here. Don't slow down, just look."

He looked, even though his head was bursting.

She was right, he thought. On the face of the cliff, about eight feet down, you could make out the edge of two long, straight stones. You could even see the edge of the one they were roofed with, which had fallen making two triangles, like an inverted letter N. Now that you saw it you could pick it out.

"You are right!" he said. "You are right!" He felt the excitement rising in himself. He was nearly convinced. All the searching over the years had left him skeptical; all the old documents, the maps, the stones. He thought of the boys. He had thought so much about them that he had had to drink a lot to forget about them. That's why his head was bursting.

"If it wasn't for those boys," she said, "we could be going at it now."

"You made a mistake," he said. "You should have taken them off the island, and then we could have come back when it all died down."

"No! No!" she said. "I am not going to have everything ruined now, just when it is in our hands."

"How can we do anything," he asked, "while all this

searching is going on? Helicopters, boats, search planes. What will they think of us? How about the way their parents are suffering?"

"If they were good parents," she said, "they wouldn't have left them roaming free like that. They should have kept their eyes on them. It will all die down, I tell you, all the searching, all the excitement."

"And what happens then?" he asked.

"We will be gone," she said. "We can deny them. It is only their word against ours."

"You are letting this thing change you altogether, Agnes," he said.

"I am not changed," she said. "I have worked hard for this all the long years. I have solved it. I have my hands almost on it. Am I to let it all go now, for the sake of a lot of stupid boys? Go on, Captain."

He headed in toward the island. He was disturbed. He wondered how the boys had fared. What could they have eaten? He was jumpy. The situation was unreal. Normally Agnes and I are decent people, he thought. We wouldn't hurt a fly. And yet she seemed to be merciless in this.

He ran the boat onto the pebbly beach in the little bay. He put out buffers, because the tide was ebbing and would soon be flowing again. He tied off a long line fore and aft.

"I will stay here," she said. "You go and see them. Find out what they know. They should be more willing to talk now. Then come back and we'll talk about it."

He walked slowly from the little bay, reluctantly. He didn't know what he would find. He just knew that they were still there, that they hadn't been found. They had told the searchers that there was no sign of the boys on the island, so all the searchers had given it a wide berth.

He walked onto the grass of the big saucer field. He stopped there and looked about him. There was no sign of life. They would be in a shelter, he thought then. Probably in the cell, which was the only real cover on the island.

He reached it and bent at the rectangular opening, not blocking it entirely with his body so that light shone into it. He made out the figures of the three boys. They looked awful, he thought, his heart dropping, like victims of a concentration camp. He counted them. There were only three.

"Well, now," he said. "Where is the little fellow? What has happened to the little fellow?"

They didn't answer him, just kept looking at him from white faces. He wondered how a little over twenty-four hours could make them look so bad. He clenched his hands. They would have to find some solution for the boys. He would have to force some solution on her.

Just then, he heard her calling. He turned to look. She was running toward him across the green field, her long tweed skirt flapping about her thin legs.

"Captain! Captain!" she was calling. "There is a boat coming in from the mainland with men in it. They must be searchers. Are they there, those boys?"

"Yes," he said.

"Then don't let them come out. Whatever happens don't let them out! Do you hear me?"

"I hear you," he said.

"I'll go back and talk to them," she said. "I'll put them off."

"All right," he said.

"Captain," she reiterated, "they must not see those boys!"

"All right, Agnes, all right!" he said impatiently.

Then she turned and went back quickly toward the bay.

George made a dive for freedom.

He did it impulsively. He thought, if I can get out and run, they cannot catch me. The captain will follow me and then Conor and Edwin can run in different directions, and we will be free. All we have to do is shout and we will be free. There was a space between the captain's legs and the opening. He dived head first toward that, meaning to do a roll and a jump to the right and get free.

So he dived.

And the minute he moved the other two jumped at the captain.

It should have worked.

But the captain was very fast.

He swung his right arm at the two boys coming from inside. He had a very strong right arm. It was like a big club. It threw them back from where they had come, breathless and hurt. His left hand reached out and caught George's ankle and pulled his whole body toward him. He clapped his right hand over his face and squeezed his mouth, and then sat with his back to the opening of the cell. Even if they had been stronger, the two inside would have needed dynamite to move him.

He pulled George's face up to his own.

He was very strong. He was hurting George. His face was grim. Normally it would be a jolly face, fat and cheerful, with a small stub nose. Now his eyes were red-rimmed and fierce.

"Don't do a thing like that again," he said. "Just don't do a thing like that again."

It was the first time George had ever been spoken to like this, or looked at like this, or assaulted like this, and it frightened him.

Then the captain brought up his other hand and rubbed at George's cheeks. Then he looked at the white on his fingers.

"So," he said. "So!" very grimly. "Get in there," he said then, "and stay there." He practically threw George in. George pulled himself over to where the other two were and sat beside them. The captain came in. He sat down opposite them. It was gloomy in there now. They couldn't see his face. There was no need to.

"I was feeling sorry for you," he said. "Real sorry. Even worrying about what your parents must be feeling for you. I don't feel sorry now. I don't trust you anymore. I don't feel sorry for you anymore. Now there is one thing I want to know. Where is the little fellow?"

None of them answered him.

"You'll tell me," he said. "You'll tell me before the day is over."

"We will not tell you," said Edwin. "We'll never tell you."

"Oh, you will," said the captain. "You will."

Their mouths were stubborn, he saw. But he was angry. He knew they had hidden the little fellow somewhere. He hoped that he wouldn't be seen by the searchers. If he was, all was lost.

"I'm going to find out," he said. "I'm going to find out before very long. Now, where did you hide the little fellow?"

They were stubbornly silent.

And Babo was getting tired of playing jackstones.

chapter

8

"We were here at the time," Agnes said. "If they had come near here we would have seen them, and brought them home, of course."

"No oars," the man said. "There should have been oars. If all else was destroyed the oars would have floated in."

"Blown out, maybe, blown out," she said.

"No," he almost shouted. "They would have drifted in with the tides. Not an oar, not even a piece of torn canvas from the boat. I know they are somewhere, somewhere. They are not at the bottom of the sea."

Babo had heard voices in the distance and the sound of boots hitting the stones.

He remained silent, crouched up in his little cavern.

It was the thought of the woman that made him cower. He was afraid of that woman.

Then Babo could not hear any more sounds, but the idea of other people on the island brought him out of his hiding place. He looked, and there was nobody there. They had gone around the near headland. He forgot all about Conor's injunctions to him to stay hidden until they called him. He set off along the shore after the voices.

He was diverted on the way by a scuttling crab in a pool. He got a piece of stone and tried to stir the crab from his hiding place. He did so. The crab ran across and under another small rock. He lifted that and he ran again. Babo was laughing at the antics of the crab.

Then he left him and wandered on again. By now he had forgotten why he came out of his hiding place. He felt hungry, so he knocked off two more limpets, cleaned them, and ate them, his small sharp teeth cutting the gristle-like meat of the limpet and chewing it.

When he was around the headland, he heard the engine of a boat. He remembered how the boys had hidden from the sound like that this morning, so he crouched down behind a rock and didn't move until the sound of the engine was very faint.

The tide was fully out now, so he could walk under the cliff of the first head. Then he came to the sandy bay where they had landed after the storm.

He played here for a little time with the sand, making heaps of it and knocking them down. He got tired of that and he went on.

He saw the cruiser lying on its side in the next little bay.

He walked toward it.

If they had had binoculars in the lobster boat that was heading for the faraway mainland, they could have seen him.

He pulled at the rope that was holding the boat. It was slack. He went closer to the boat. He heard no sound from it. He went to the low side, where it was lying toward him, inviting him into it, it seemed. He reached up and caught the sides and looked in. He had to stand on his toes, so he went and got a few small rocks and piled them and stood on those, and he was quite high and could throw a leg over the side. He did so.

Now he stood in the well. Opposite him was a small platform in front of the wheel and a tall gear lever. Balancing himself, he reached for this and joggled it.

There was a door on his right and a door on his left with brass handles. He crawled over to the right-side door and put his hand on the handle and pulled and it opened. He was looking into a cabin with a table and seats on each side, but what caught his attention was the sight of the food on the table. It had slid down and was held by the raised edge. Babo could even smell it. A fresh loaf of bread he saw, just like the one he would buy for his mother from the shop and pick little holes out of it with his fingers, so when he went home his mother would say, "What? Have the mice been at the bread again?"

Babo went on into the cabin, having to clutch on to the table since the whole cabin was at an angle.

He put his hand on the loaf. He saw beside the loaf a

round can. On the can was a picture of meat. He pulled the can to him and then he saw a rectangular package that he recognized. It was a pound of butter. He put that with the can and the loaf.

He didn't reason it out, but he saw a lot of big papers on the table, so he put the loaf and the can and the package into the middle of all the big papers and bundled the rest of the papers around them, and there under his hand, under the papers, was a long piece of red string, so Babo took this red string and wrapped it around the mouth of the bundle, and tied two big knots in it. He was well able to tie knots. His mother was always scolding him for tying knots in the cord of the window blind, in the laces of loose shoes, in the cat's tail if he would let him.

Now he had his bundle, so he came out again, closed the door after him, clambered over the side, and set off back the way he had come.

And this is the funny thing. It was only when he was back near the hiding place that it entered his head that he should never have left it. And he remembered what Conor had said to him and that Conor would be angry with him because he had left, so he went in there again and sat, fairly patiently, waiting for Conor to come for him, nursing the bundle in his arms.

Agnes came up to the captain.

"It's all right, they are gone," she said. "They stayed quiet for you?"

"They stayed quiet," he said, coming out of the cell. "There was nothing else they could do. They are a bunch of tricksters, those dear little boys. Do you know they had whitened their faces so that we would think they were dying? There was no sight of the little fellow?"

"No," she said. "He's not with them?"

"No," he said. "They have him hidden. I was waiting every minute to hear a shout."

"We saw no sign of him," she said. "They searched the shore. It was the father of the dangerous one. He won't give up."

"What will we do now, so?" he asked.

"We'll go back," she said. "Leave them here. They are quite safe. They must have found food some way. Let them go on finding it."

"I don't feel as soft about them now as I did," said the captain.

"We'll go back home," she said. "We will talk it over there, and try and resolve the position. Now that the others have searched the island, they won't be back. So we have time. Let them stew here for another while."

"Is there any way they can communicate with the shore?" the captain asked. "I wouldn't trust them."

"There is no way," she said. "Leave them. We can see the island as well as anybody else. We have the fastest boat. We can be here first."

She walked away.

The captain bent and looked in at them.

"Good-bye, boys," he said. "Enjoy your camping trip.

By the time we come back, I'm sure you will be in a better position to talk."

They didn't answer him, so he rose and followed after his wife. By the time they reached the boat the tide was coming in, and the water had covered the stones Babo had used to get on the boat, so they went aboard as soon as she was afloat, drew in the lines, backed out, and because it was some time before either of them went into the cabin, they didn't know of the havoc that the little boy had wrought.

The boys stood outside the cell and looked after the two. They started to wipe the white from their faces with their hands.

"That wasn't a very bright idea," said George ruefully.

"It could have been good," said Edwin consolingly.

"Why did it madden him so much?" Conor asked.

"I don't know," said George. "I'll never understand grown-up people."

"That woman is a bit crazy," said Edwin.

"That makes it worse," said George.

"You heard what she said. My father was here," said Conor. "My father will never give up."

"If only he had found Babo," said George.

"Babo! Oh, poor Babo," said Conor, and he ran toward the far shore. The others followed him.

"At least," said George, "they didn't get to frighten Babo. I'm glad we hid him."

"I'm beginning to get afraid of those two," said Edwin.

"Don't they seem very ruthless?"

"They just seem crazy to me," said George. "They will have to let us go sometime. And then they'll get it in the neck."

"That's what I'm afraid of," said Edwin. "That they know that."

"Cheer up," said George, clapping him on the shoulder. "We'll have fish for dinner when we catch them."

"Look! Look! Look!" Conor was calling to them, holding up the bundle. "Look what Babo has!"

They were amazed.

"Where on earth did he get that? Here, Babo, where did you get the bundle?" George asked him, bending to face him.

"Boat," said Babo. "I went to the boat."

"Open it," said Edwin. "See what's in it."

Conor pulled at the string. It was well knotted, so he had to pull it over the papers. He placed them on the shore and the three of them got down on their knees and goggled at the contents.

"Bread," said George, putting his nose close to it.

"And butter," shouted Edwin, almost screaming.

"And a can of corned beef," said Conor, completely amazed.

They looked down and they looked up, and then they looked at Babo. And George raised his hands in the air and prostrated himself before him three times, saying: "All hail, Ali Babo!"

"What a beautiful thief," said Edwin reverently.

Babo started to laugh at George, and jumped around shouting, "Ali Babo! Ali Babo!"

Conor was doing the practical thing; he was trying to open the can with the blade of the small knife. It was difficult. Finally, he pierced it and went around with the blade of the knife, driving it with a stone, so he could lift off the top, and then shake out the round-shaped meat onto a stone.

"Just smell it! Just smell it!" said Edwin.

"Oh, boy," said George. "Ali Babo, you are a genius." He hugged Babo.

They sat and ate. They could think of nothing else. They managed to slice the bread and coat it with the creamery butter, and over that put a slice of the red and yellow meat, and they ate it almost ecstatically. It even silenced their talk.

It was Conor who, shifting his position, kicked at the papers that Babo had used to carry the food, and suddenly stopped eating, stopped chewing as he looked. Then he swallowed his mouthful with a gulp and said, "Look! Look! This is it! This is the map I saw. I swear it. And all those other papers. This is the secret. Now we know. He not only got away with the food, but he brought along the secret of the island. You hear? You hear that, Babo? You know what you have done?"

"Are you sure?" Edwin asked.

"I'm positive," said Conor. "Look for yourself."

They looked at one another. Their hearts were beating

fast. George thought, maybe we shouldn't look. Maybe we should remain in a state of ignorance.

But it was too late.

Edwin was reaching for the map and the papers, and it wouldn't be long before they knew everything, for better or worse.

chapter
9

They looked first at the map. They could make nothing at all of it.

"And yet it must be obvious," said Edwin, "if they thought Conor would know what it was just with one look."

They studied it.

"It looks like a map of a place I should know," said Conor finally, "but I can't get it into my thick head."

"What do they mean impression of a stone?" George asked.

"Let's look at these other papers," said Edwin. "Maybe they will make sense to us."

"There's a lot of them," said Conor.

There was quite a sheaf of papers, written in pencil and clipped together. Edwin sorted them and started reading.

"Come on," said George, "read it out loud. Don't keep it to yourself."

"It's hard to read," said Edwin. "It's as if it were written by four spiders. Give me time to get the hang of it."

They waited for him, looking over his shoulder.

Then he read for them haltingly:

"'Oh, this family of the Maelrua, what feckless Irishmen they were, possessing nothing after two thousand years except a decrepit house and a few acres of parkland, and a cellar stuffed with old lore and the wrack of the centuries. When I met the captain he had talked of his estates in the west of Ireland and his desire one day to retire to them. Well, when we married and he did retire to them, what a shock! How long it took me to put a semblance of respectability on the poor place, to eject the cunning trespassers with their excuse of broken fences and rights of way, to mend broken gutters, primitive plumbing, and starved fields. How I succeeded you can see.

"'But there was treasure in the cellar in those lead-lined trunks. By what miracle had they roused themselves from their drunken lethargy long enough to see that such things were preserved from the prevailing damp of that wet, windy climate?

"'For they *were* noble people. They went back as far as the spoken word, as the old manuscripts proved, the buried traditions handed on with a jest. After two years in that cellar, I emerged with three things:

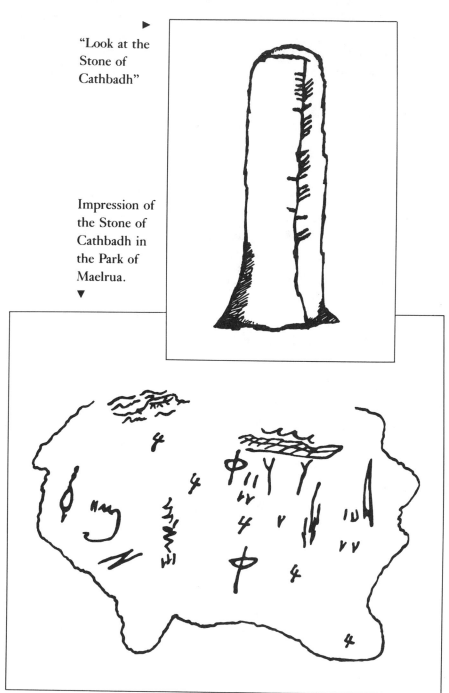

"Look at the Stone of Cathbadh"

Impression of the Stone of Cathbadh in the Park of Maelrua.

"'1. The transcript, faded beyond belief, written with blackberry juice, I would say, of the big story in their lives which had happened *fourteen hundred years* ago, and to which they paid not the slightest attention.

"'2. The upright stone near what they called the Fairy Fort in the sea field with the faint traces of Ogham writing carved on its sides.

"'3. The big flat stone on the opposite side of the Fort, with the hieroglyphics carved on it, which *even now* is known as the Stone of Cathbadh.

"'Many distinguished archaeologists had come to examine the stone. It had been photographed, written about in learned tomes for two hundred years. It had been measured, and the stupid government was even talking about removing the stone and putting it in a museum. Well, they can put it in a museum now if they wish to, and how stupid those learned archaeologists were not to discover the secret of the stone, and it placed right there on a slope overlooking the great bay!

"'As for the upright stone, it threw them into the same state of awe. Because it was a purely pagan stone, so it must date before the era of Christianity. They could not interpret it, except to say that the weathered Ogham writing probably meant that this was the stone of Cathbadh.

"'I knew that Ogham writing was a sort of cryptographic carving based on the Irish alphabet, and used solely by the druids and kept a close secret by them, in order to gain wealth with hocus pocus. The more words they had to inscribe, the more they had to be paid.

"'But it struck me that this was different. It didn't say the right words. I stared at it for months, as if it had a message for me, and it had. One day it seemed that it was not a burial stone of Cathbadh, but rather that it seemed to say: *Look at the Stone of Cathbadh.*

"'So I went and stared at the Stone of Cathbadh, and one day it too seemed to have a message for me.'"

"I know! I know!" suddenly Conor shouted. "I thought it looked to me like something I knew, the map, I mean, and what is it but a map of the bay. See! Look at it."

"Shh, Conor," said George. "Go on, Edwin."

Edwin continued:

"'It was a bright, sunny day. The sun was shining on the stone and it was shining on the bay which I could see lying under my eyes, and suddenly I thought, this is like a primitive map of the bay out there. And then I knew it was, that it couldn't possibly be anything else!'"

"Now there, wasn't I right?" Conor asked excitedly.

"Calm down, Conor," said George. "Go on, Edwin."

"'And then there was the manuscript of the old folktale called Ranna an Rioghs—Verses of the King. In it was a mention of the Clan Maelrua, which was why it was kept over the centuries, not really all that old, several hundred years old, and it was obviously copied from older manuscripts, but now, with this extra knowledge, what a significance it acquired! It entailed for me the learning of this ancient tongue. I could have got it translated by a scholar, but that would entail his knowing its contents. This would be dangerous. So I entered on the great task myself. It took me four years. But when I managed to translate the significant passages, the three treasures were linked. This is the passage from the old tale:

"'. . . so after that the High King was in a depression and a severe sickness and a wonderful great vomit of heart's sickness burst out through his mouth, it behooved the noble druid Cathbadh with his faithful followers to flee into Connacht, carrying with them the sacred gods, because the princes were taken and ensnared in the new religion of the Christians, and in all the land there was but the Maelrua who followed the right old way and gave honor to the gods of his fathers.

"'So Cathbadh the druid had fled to the land of the Maelrua, *carrying with him the sacred gods*. This was significant, for earlier mention had been made of the Golden Ox of Cathbadh. What could this be? Later, the tale went on:

"'. . . and the Maelrua falling sick with fever and bone pain put the word on Cathbadh and he came to him and the Maelrua spoke to him in this manner: My master Cathbadh, he said, I have great cause and reason to be sick, for the four great provinces of Ireland will come and destroy my stronghold and my forts, my ridge-hills in lowlands and in valleys, they will burn my fastnesses, and my good homesteads, they will take from me my lands and my women and my youths, and they will take from me too my cows and my herds of constant milk and my beautiful foreign seeds, my heavy broadside hogs and my choice fighting bulls, without provocation from me, only that I shelter the noble druid and his followers and give honor to the gods of our fathers.

"'Cathbadh answered him and this is what he said: If they do these things, he said, then it will bring great honor to you and pleasure to the gods. You are a noble leader.

"'But Maelrua said to him: What is the weight of honor against life, and you have tried with all your great knowing to cure me of the fever that torments me, but it is not so and now I must send messengers and envoys forthwith to those Christians to come and heal me and wet me with their water so that I may gain my life, and keep my people safe from the edge of the sword.

"'And Cathbadh the noble druid wept for his weakness and said: It is a great sadness to me, O Maelrua, that you are not steadfast in your faith and that I must abandon your shelter with my people, because until the sky falls the gods are my gods, if we are the last ones in the great provinces to hold them. And we will go now and offer you the thanks of the gods for the shelter you have accorded us to this date.

"'And Maelrua wept bitter tears and said: It is a great sorrow to me that you will do this thing, but I will hold you in honor for it, and he wept and he wept again, so he was like to flood his chamber with tears, but Cathbadh went and gathered together his people, his handmaidens and his treasures and the Great Yellow Ox, and with the people bowing and crying they departed on the ship from the shore and they sailed into the great sea, and the people stood on the cliffs and they wept and bewailed, but it little availed them crying: Do not leave us, noble Cathbadh. Do not sail away into the unknown with the Golden Ox. How can we live without the god? Come back to us!

"'But Cathbadh sailed away out into the sun, and some said they sailed until the sun swallowed them and they were never again seen by the eyes of the world, and none knew of them ever again except for the signs they left after them of their going, which can be seen by many, even to the present day, but the Maelrua lived long, and they did not devastate him. He was a great chieftain and died in a great age, having secured his possessions forever by the water of the Christians, but when he died at last they said that his words were: O Cathbadh! O noble Cathbadh, that I should have sent you to the edge of the world with the golden god.

"'So it came to me that the gods of Cathbadh were not just dreams, or intangibles. They were real, real, real! When they talked of golden gods, they meant just that: *gold*. And here was I with all the clues if I could only solve them. They were under my eyes. I could *see* the Great Yellow Ox. It was somewhere, somewhere, somewhere and it belonged to me because I was the only one in fifteen hundred years to see the significance of those three things.

"'We combed every island in the great bay for signs, but of course there were none. Fifteen hundred years of weather alone would cover any traces of habitation. But I went back to the stone map again and scratched it and cleaned it, and then, up in the left corner, what had seemed to be just insignificant scratches suddenly emerged as seven lines. I remember the trembling fit that came over me when I deciphered the scratches. They were like this:

and what could that be but the primitive illustration of an animal, of an *ox*; and looking more closely at what looked like five figure 4's leading straight out to the last island, an island of two heads, what could they be but signs of ships heading in the direction of the island on which was the sign of an *ox*. It seemed so clear. Scholars had said it was a record of a battle, with soldiers in clans and footprints of men, but here it was as clear to me as if Cathbadh was talking into my ear. I *knew* and I was the only one who knew, and when I saw the signs on the cliff face of the head, I knew beyond doubt that the burial chamber of Cathbadh was on this island, and that I would soon have my hands on the Great Yellow Ox. Mine! Nobody else's. Here is a secret hidden for a thousand and a half years, and I have uncovered it. I have. Nobody else's. So to me belongs the mantle of Cathbadh. To me and nobody else. And all he possessed. All the sufferings he went through to keep the golden gods from the hands of the Christians, all these I too will regard as a sacred duty. Nobody will interfere with me, nobody at all. I will get them and I will hold them and nobody on the face of the earth will be allowed to interfere with my possessing them.'"

There was a silence between them when Edwin's voice ceased. They put away the papers and they got the big map and stretched it out in front of them, and the three boys got on their knees and traced the things she had written about.

"It's just like an adventure story," said Conor.

"Listen," said George, "she must be nuts. I can't see all the things she says in this."

Babo had been playing away from them, on his own. The things that were being read bored him. So he went off exploring the pools. But now he was back beside Conor. He forced his small hand into Conor's hand, and

Conor looked up at him impatiently, but then saw the direction of his eyes, and looked up and slowly got to his feet when he saw over his head, on the high ground, the captain and his lady looking down at them.

He got to his feet, and Babo went around behind him, holding his legs.

Conor coughed.

"Hey, lads, lads," he said.

They looked at him and then looked where he was looking and slowly got to their feet.

The lady spoke to them.

"You monsters," she said. "You despicable monsters!" Then the two started to come down to them.

The boys didn't move.

chapter
10

She snatched the papers from Edwin's hand.
"Stupid boy," she said. "Ruffian. Fool. What kind
of people do you come from that you will read the private
papers of other people?" She bent to the ground and
picked up the map. She folded it carefully. She pointed
at Conor. "It's all your fault," she said, "for the predicament that you are in now. You are like all your people,
nosy peasants, can't keep your fingers out of other
people's soup. You even have the little monster trained to
steal."

She moved toward them. Babo dug his head into
Conor's back and George and Edwin went close to
Conor.

"You leave him alone," said Conor, angrily. "You are a
monster yourself, ma'am, that won't let us go from this
island."

"Shut up!" she said ferociously. They thought she was going to hit Conor. He was bracing himself for a blow.

"I don't want you," she said then, dropping her hand. "Any of you. It was an evil day for me the day you stuck your nose into my business. Even yet it might have been all right, if you hadn't sent that urchin to rob and steal so you could learn more than you should. Now you have left me no alternative. I will have to keep you. But I can tell you that you will be sorry for what you have done. Get up to the cell now, and stay there until I want you. Go on! Move!"

They looked at her. Conor thought there was terrible dislike in her eyes. He bent down and Babo climbed onto his back and kept his head buried in his shoulders. Babo didn't want to look at the angry lady. He wasn't used to such treatment, Conor thought. All the ladies took one look at the tow-haired, chubby little boy and fell in love with him. That's what Babo was used to. But this one wouldn't even love her own baby if she had one. They moved off.

"Wait!" she called. They waited.

"Pick up the remains of the food you stole," she said, "and bring it with you. And be careful with it. It will have to last you for a long time."

Edwin and George picked up the remains of the bread and the can of meat and the butter. They looked very meek, but they weren't. George was raging. He wasn't used to being spoken to like this. Neither was Edwin, for that matter; his parents would spend hours reasoning with him about something he had done, or was about to do, or contemplated doing. Neither had known before that there were people like the Lady Agnes in the world.

They tramped back to the cell. The captain walked beside them, humming something, picking at his white teeth with a sliver of wood. He spoke once. "Smart boys," he said, shaking his head. "Such smart boys."

Then they were at the cell.

"In," he said, pointing at the opening with his tooth-pick. "And stay in until I tell you to come out."

They went in silently and sat down on the bed of bracken. At least it was cooler in the stone cell than it was outside.

The woman came up and stood beside the captain.

"Well, now," he said.

"You stay here," she said. "I'll go back and collect enough supplies; everything we will need. I will be two or three hours. We can get to work tomorrow. We will have to work fast now. The weather will have to break in a few days. It would be as well to be finished and away before it does break."

"I'd better go with you," he said.

"No," she said. "They must not be allowed out of our sight for a minute anymore. I don't trust them an inch. You never know what they will get up to. It was a great pity that the storm didn't finish them. But they are only another obstacle. We have overcome so many that we will get past them too."

"All right," he said, and sat on a stone. At least, he thought, she has gotten over the fury that possessed her when she had gone to the cabin and found that the papers and the map had vanished. He thought she wouldn't have been as upset if he himself had been swept overboard.

"Go back! Go back!" she had called to him. "They have the map and the papers. Do you hear that? They have the map and the papers."

He couldn't believe it. "They were under our eyes all the time," he said.

"Not the little one, not that little fox," she said.

"How could he do a thing like that?" he asked. "Isn't he only as big as a button?"

"But sly, sly, sly, like all the rest of them," she cried. "Get back there. We must get our hands on these papers before they get a chance to destroy them or hide them. If they do, I'll kill them! I'll kill them!"

"Agnes! Agnes!" he said. "Don't get so excited. The damage is done. Even if they destroy them or hide them, what does it matter now? We know where we are going and what we have to do."

She sat on the bench. She unclenched her hands.

"What a terrible thing," she said. "You know all the years of striving that I put into this. No other eye, no other brain, but mine. And now these grubby boys have their hands on these papers. My papers. Reading them! They were meant for no eyes but my own. I could wipe them out, just plain wipe them out. Children never appealed to me. Never! Now I know why. I must have been anticipating this day and known the utter wretchedness of them."

"Calm yourself," he said. "It's not worth the worry. If we have a lot of digging to do, can't we use them? Think of it that way." He was bringing the boat around in a circle. The sea was calm. It was too calm. The sound of the engine would travel a long distance.

"There's that," she said. "There is that. You are practical, Captain. It is one of your best qualities. What if they hear us coming?"

"With luck they won't," he said, throttling down the engine. They were fairly close to the island. He turned away off to the left of it, since whatever faint gusts of gentle winds that were in it were coming down from the mountains behind them. So he crept up on the island from the west of it, with the engine barely turning over. She was looking at the island through binoculars.

"I can see no sign of them," she said.

"Good," he said. "They are probably wolfing down the food. They won't hear the engine over the sound of their own jaws."

They came in on the flowing tide and tied up the cruiser. Then they walked slowly and carefully to the center of the green field. They looked toward the cell and saw no one, then they listened and faintly heard the voice. They moved toward it, closer and closer. The captain could see the muscles tighten on her jaws as she started to understand the words. They stopped still, until the voice of Edwin ceased and they heard the comments of the others and then they stepped forward.

"You were very careless, boys," the captain said conversationally when he heard the sound of the engine at full power retreating from the island. "What you should have done was read the papers and then put them back somehow. You will never be crafty. But you did a good job of training the little one. He'll make an excellent thief."

They didn't answer him.

He rose and stretched himself.

"You can come out now," he said, "and do what you like, within reason of course. If you would like to all get into the sea and swim to the mainland, you are welcome. I would be very pleased. It's only ten miles or so, and there are good, strong currents."

There was no reply to his taunting.

"I said come out of there," he said harshly then.

They rose from their sitting and came out. He had his hands on his hips.

"We'd better be friends, boys," he said. "Since we are going to be together for a little while. Just do what you are told, that's all, and behave yourselves. You know, I was a real captain. I was even captain of a sailing ship once. I have had many tough crews under me. I was always able to handle them. I knew their twisted thoughts, even before they knew them themselves. I am up to all the tricks, so just behave yourselves and you will have as much freedom as you want. Remember that." He was smiling at them, then he turned and walked toward the head that was the cliff over the sea, and when he reached it he went down on his belly and looked over and stayed looking over, examining it critically.

"Now what are we going to do?" Conor asked.

George was bending down to Babo.

"You know something, Babo," he said. "You are a

great man. It was the best day's work we ever did to bring you with us. Isn't that true, you men?"

"That's true," said Edwin. "We should make Babo leader of this expedition."

"Hear that, Babo?" said George.

Babo was pleased with the praise. He had been crying a little, George saw. His face with streaked. Now he smiled and put his arms around George's neck.

"I don't know how," said George, "but we are going to get out of this somehow."

"The white stones," said Edwin.

"What white stones?" Conor asked.

"You know. Those white marble-looking stones, all over the shore," said Edwin. "The round quartz-looking ones."

"Yes," said Conor.

"Let's gather them," said Edwin. "Look, that helicopter might come back. It's been out every morning. Let's go and collect the stones one by one, casually, and we'll drop them over there on the grass, and make them form the word HELP. If we do it right they will never know we have done it."

"That woman has eyes like a hawk," said George.

"And the captain is not dumb," said Conor.

"We'll try anyhow," said Edwin. "He can't keep his eyes on the four of us at once. We might get away with it."

"Let's go," said George. He kept Babo with him, holding his hand. So they went in three directions.

The white stones were not easy to find, but all the

same there were quite a few of them. There were a lot of small ones, but the bigger sizes were scarce. When they got one they would stroll from the shore to the grass and look over toward the captain on the cliff. Sometimes he would turn his head and look toward them. The one with the stone would stand looking back at him, or else sit down despondently on the grass, plucking at it. Then he would rise and look about him, having left the stone on the ground, and gradually, over a couple of hours, until in the distance they heard the sound of the engine of the boat returning, they moved the white stones with their feet, until they spelled out, white on green, irregular, but obvious from above, the only hope they seemed to have left, the word that nobody could misunderstand.

When the cruiser was pulling in to the island the captain called them. The sun was setting in the sea. The desired mainland was beautifully colored; the mountains were a pale, misty purple.

"Into the cell and stay there," the captain said, so they went in, and, since they were hungry, they cut the rest of the bread and spread the butter and the meat on it and ate it, and they enjoyed it very much.

Before he went to sleep, Conor prayed, Please let that helicopter come.

chapter

11

The pilot swung the helicopter toward the island.
It was a brilliant morning. He and his companion
could see the whole bay below them, beautifully blue,
with no whitecaps on the water, the pattern of the fields
multicolored with ripening crops and the green grass of
the meadows, the mountains gray and brown and purple, and many lakes taking their color from the sky. Here
and there the mountains and some of the islands seemed
to be wearing skirts of white mist.

"I'm getting tired of all this, Joe," the pilot said. "We
have searched every inch and nook and corner of this
bay. What we haven't covered the boats have covered. I
tell you those kids are gone."

"How do you know?" said Joe. "I mean how do you
know for sure?"

"I have a head," said the pilot, "I have eyes, and I have

reason. If there was sight or sign of them, we would have seen something of them."

"Maybe they were picked up by a boat that was on its way to Australia," said Joe.

"I better bring you into this century," said the pilot. "There is an invention called radio. If they had been picked up, somebody would have called on the radio."

"Maybe this boat has no radio," said Joe.

"How does a small boat without radio get to go to Australia?" the pilot asked patiently.

"It's just that we have to keep hoping," said Joe.

"It's just on account of the mother of that American kid," said the pilot. "She has the government haunted. Listen, if she doesn't get back her boy, even his body, I can tell you that the United States of America will have to declare war on Ireland."

"That would be an interesting possibility," said Joe. "Do you think we would be able to beat them?"

"I can't understand," said the pilot, "how any parents could let their kids go out on a bay in one of the worst storms in twenty years. I just can't understand it."

"How many kids do you have, Pat?" Joe asked.

"None," said Pat, "because I don't happen to be married."

"Ah, I see," said Joe.

"What is that profound 'Ah' supposed to mean?" Pat asked. "Do you have to have kids to understand this thing? How many have you?"

"Eight," said Joe, "and I can tell you that you'd want

four hundred eyes in your head to watch them. They dart around like ants when you lift a stone."

"I'm not hard-hearted," said Pat. "I'm just tired. I don't like to think of four kids waving away under that sea with the weed. But we have to be sensible. They are gone."

"Then where are their bodies?" Joe asked. "Where are the remains of their boat? Where are the oars?"

"You have been brainwashed by the father of the Irish boy," said Pat. "That's what's wrong with you. Well, let's keep looking, for all the good it will do us. Oh, there's that captain chap. Their cruiser is there. They must have spent the night on the island. He's waving to us. Hello, Captain. What wouldn't I give to be like those, with plenty of money and a nice cruiser, just mooching about, sleeping where they like. Having fun."

"I'd say he's henpecked," said Joe, waving at the stocky figure that was waving up to them. "See his wife. Sour as a crab apple."

"He's tough," said Pat. "He could knock her into the middle of next week."

Then they were over the sea, and they had not seen the white stones crying HELP. They had not seen them, because they were not there. At least they weren't crying, as the boys saw when they emerged from the cell.

The helicopter was far away toward the mainland when they came out. When Conor heard the sound first he saw that Edwin was awake and they looked at one another and made a rush for the opening. They didn't get far because right outside were the captain's legs. So they sat and waited and listened to the helicopter, very loud and then not so loud as it chopped its way through the air. When they couldn't hear it clearly the captain moved away from them, back toward the boat, without a glance at them. They waited. They shook George awake. "The helicopter was here," they told him. That brought George wide awake. They walked into the sunlight and sauntered toward the place where they had placed the stones.

They looked stunned, at the neat way they had been kicked together in four heaps, into meaningless piles of white stones.

They heard the captain laughing.

He was at the other end of the field, near the bay of the boat.

"He found them," said George. "Look at him. If only there was something we could do to him."

The captain had stopped laughing. He was now waving at them to come to him. They had to obey. He stood there waiting for them with his hands on his hips.

"That wasn't a good trick, boys," he said. "If you had to do it you should have done it when it was dark. Do you want breakfast?"

They didn't answer him.

"If you want breakfast you will have to work for it," he said. "There are stores on the boat that must be unloaded. When you have done that and have worked hard we will see about getting you something to eat."

He turned and walked on.

They looked at one another. Would they work or wouldn't they? They smelled something then. It was frying bacon, coming from the direction of the cruiser. Frying bacon on the clear morning air.

The three of them walked toward the boat.

For the next hour, they worked hard. They unloaded a bag with a tent and posts and a folding cot. They erected this within two feet of the opening of the cell. "That is so that I can be near you and keep an eye on you," said the captain, smiling at them broadly. When Babo woke up and came out rubbing his eyes, the captain went to the boat and came back with a large colored beach ball, which he threw to him. This surprised them all, including Babo, who looked at the enticing ball with a mixture of suspicion and attraction. They watched him. He walked away from it, keeping his eyes on it. Then he would move a few steps closer to it. Then he would look at the captain again and walk away from it. But finally it proved too attractive and he went to it and gave it a hearty kick, and, forgetting everything else, gave a shout and followed after it.

"Back to work," said the captain.

They unloaded two pickaxes, two shovels, a crowbar, several lengths of thick rope, a rope ladder, and thick plastic buckets, black ones, and they carted all this stuff to the far head.

Then they brought a cylinder of bottled gas from the boat and an attachment on it that made it like a stove, and they put this in front of the tent, and the captain put a skillet on it and fried bacon and eggs and sausages on the skillet, and boiled water in a kettle and made tea, and the Lady Agnes, not speaking a word to them, came up with bread and cut it and buttered it and gave them plastic plates and cups from a basket.

By this time the boys were very hungry, and if they had any notion of not accepting *anything* from the hands of these people, they soon forgot all about it and ate the food. Babo ate his food sitting on the beach ball.

The Lady Agnes took a big leather-covered tape measure and went back up to the head. She bent over the cliff and looked, and she measured a space back from the cliff about four feet wide, marking it with rope.

The captain was smoking a cigar.

"Boys," he said, leaning back on his elbow. "I have something to say to you." He watched them from under his black eyebrows.

They looked at him suspiciously, saying nothing, slowly chewing the last of the food.

"There are lots of ways we could do this," he said to them. "We could, for example, do it the hard way, put you all into that cell there and block up the opening with good, heavy stones. This way you would be no problem, and we could forget you. Don't think I won't do that if I have to."

He puffed smoke at the air. His eyes were hard. They knew well he was capable of doing a thing like that.

"On the other hand," he said, "you are boys and this is a great adventure. Is it possible for you to see it this way? You have read books about treasure hunts? Well, what's this but one? Somewhere under that cliff there is a long tunnel, and at the end of it there is a round chamber, and in that chamber there is treasure that has not seen the light of day for well over a thousand years. Imagine that? Can't you see that? Right. We dig and we find the tunnel, and we dig and we find the chamber, and we shine a light in there and what will we see?"

"How do you know," asked Edwin, "that somebody else hasn't been there before you? It's been a long time."

"That's part of the adventure," said the captain. "It's the gamble that makes it attractive. If we knew for sure there was something there, there wouldn't be any pounding of the pulses."

"Listen," said George, "why didn't you tell us all this from the beginning and ask us to help? It would have been fun."

"If you knew and you were free to talk, the whole world would know," said the captain. "This discovery belongs to my wife, Agnes. It was her genius that figured it out. It belongs to her."

"All these ancient things belong to the nation," said Edwin precisely.

"All these things belong to whoever discovers them," said the captain. "And don't you forget it."

"Suppose there's nothing there," said Conor.

"Then it is all over," said the captain, "and we all laugh and go home."

"We'll go home," said George, "but we won't be laughing."

"You shouldn't say things like that," said the captain

softly. "My wife wouldn't like to hear you saying things like that."

"And what happens if there is treasure there and you find it?" Edwin asked.

The captain looked away toward where his wife was measuring. This thought disturbed him. What would she do? How would she react? It was so disturbing that when it woke him at night and he stared into the darkness he had to get up and drink rum to make himself forget it.

"We'll see," he said, rising to his feet. He poured the hot water from the kettle into a bucket. "Make everything shipshape now," he said. "Wash the cups and plates and let the sun dry them."

He went off toward his wife.

The boys went to wash the plates and cups and knives and forks.

"What do we do now?" George asked.

"I don't know," said Conor.

"We do what we are told," said Edwin. "What can we do?"

"Do you really think they'd shut us up in the cell?" Conor asked.

"I'd say yes," said Edwin.

"So would I," said George.

"So we will have to help them?" said Conor.

"It might not be bad, at that," said George. "Maybe there is a lot of stuff there. What would it be?"

"Gods and stuff," said Edwin. "Maybe skeletons."

"Good grief," said Conor, "I don't want to see any old skeleton."

"It might be interesting," said Edwin.

Babo was playing with the ball, kicking it and following it and throwing it up in the air. They watched him.

"Wouldn't it be nice to be that young?" said Edwin.

"I wouldn't mind so much if Babo wasn't with us," said Conor.

"Yeah," said George. "It might be tough on Babo."

"When you are that age," said Edwin wisely, "you don't know what's going on."

"I hope not," said Conor.

"We'd better go now," said Edwin. "The captain is calling us."

They started to walk toward the head.

"We'll have to take the first chance we get," said George. "Suppose we started to run now? Would we get to the boat in time to have it on the water before they caught up with us?"

"No," said Edwin, "we'd have to gather Babo first, and they would be on to us in a flash."

"Besides," said Conor, "don't you see what the woman is carrying on her shoulder now?"

They looked as they walked.

"What is it she has on her shoulder?" George asked.

"It's a shotgun," said Conor. "Can't you see it?"

"Wow!" said George. "A shotgun!"

"Well," said Edwin, "maybe she's not a good shot."

"You don't have to be a good shot with a shotgun,"

said George. "It spreads out like a fan. That's bad, that shotgun."

Just behind the head there was a broad hollow in the ground. In this hollow the captain had measured a space six feet long by four feet wide. He had already taken off his coat and his sleeves were rolled up on very thick and hairy arms. He was slicing the green sward with a shovel.

"This is it, boys," he said. "We will go down here, about eight feet and we should reach it."

"And hurry, hurry, hurry!" the woman said. "Come on! Come on! Get on with it! Get up those tools and dig."

The boys took an implement each and started hacking at the soft ground. Even if someone had had a telescope on the mainland and turned it on the island they could not have seen the workers because of the hollow. The scheming mind of George has assessed their situation, so he spat on his hands and dug the tip of the pickax into the grass.

chapter

12

It was easy enough for the first four feet. The soil was soft and the rocks were small. But then they started to encounter sticky yellow soil that was like glue with big round rocks embedded in it. The shovels were short handled and the deeper they went the harder it was to throw up the loosened soil, so two of the boys climbed out of the hole and, tying ropes around the handles of the buckets, lowered them to be filled, hauled them up and emptied them, and lowered them again.

The captain worked as if he had only a day left in life. He would loosen a big stone with the crowbar, then taking a deep breath, he would get his hands around it, raise it chest high and pitch it out of the hole, the tendons and veins standing out on his thick neck. "The more stones, the less dirt," he would say, but soon even he was not able to throw the stones high enough, so he went back to the boat to get some more equipment.

The boys sat on the grass looking at their blisters while they waited for him. They were glad of the rest. Their hands were sore. Their legs and trousers were dirtied from the soil. The blisters rose on their hands at the base of the fingers, and burst, and some more came out after the burst ones.

"I wouldn't mind," said George in a loud voice. "But what direction are we going in? Suppose these people built their chamber out into the cliff over the sea, and over the years the sea washed the whole thing away from the cliff?"

"Don't be stupid!" the woman said. She was pacing up and down, watching the captain going toward the boat.

"It could have happened, ma'am," said Conor.

"They had more intelligence than you," she said. "They would start their passage from the sea side and work into the hill. Otherwise why would they build the chamber at all, if the sea was to get it in a few years? Don't be stupid. Get up and do something. Don't be sitting around there doing nothing!"

"I'm hungry, lads; how about you?" Edwin asked.

"You'll get food when you have earned it," she said. She wasn't carrying the shotgun now. She had left it leaning against a stone, but she never walked too far away from it, George noticed. He had been thinking of making a dive for it, grabbing it, and holding her up. Would he shoot if she didn't do what he told her? he wondered. He didn't think he would, or would he?

Would she call his bluff if he was bluffing? He didn't know. Anyhow she had eyes like a hawk, restless eyes, not cold, but indifferent. George thought that if she had to pull the trigger she would do so.

"What's keeping him? Captain! Captain!" she called.

Edwin looked at her.

She looked like somebody's mother, he thought, if you saw her from the side. She looked like a lady with her white hair and her regal nose. It was only when she turned to face you and you saw her eyes that you wouldn't want her for your mother. She was always restless, moving about, her hands moving or her feet moving, shoving one of them away to take a bucket of earth and pull it up and empty it, or reaching for a stone with her thin blue-veined hands to pull it away from the brink.

"Hurry! Hurry! Captain!" she was calling.

"Patience, Agnes, patience," the captain said as he came toward them with the equipment over his shoulder.

This consisted of three pieces of timber, which he set over the hole like a tripod, lashing their tops together and fastening a block and pulley to them and running thick rope through the block and the pulley.

"Now," he said, and jumped back into the hole.

With Edwin and George (and sometimes the Lady Agnes) hauling, the big round stones came out easily and they could swing them free.

George was the one in the hole with the captain when they uncovered the flat stone slab.

"Hey, you guys," he shouted. "I've hit something.

Look at this! Look at this!"

He cleared around it with the shovel, and they could see it. It was standing on its side, about three feet long and three inches thick, obviously fashioned by man. It had been one of the side stones on which a similar flat roof stone would have rested.

For the first time the boys themselves were excited, particularly when they saw as George and the captain cleared it that the stone was decorated. Circles and whorls had been indented in its whole surface. The whorls had form and design.

"Listen," George shouted up at them. "Maybe all this is true."

"Get on with it! Get on with it!" the woman called. She was bending down, holding on to the tripod. "Why wouldn't it be true? It's there. It's all there like the god will be there. Get on with it!"

"Easy! Easy!" the captain said.

Soon, under their feet, they found the top stone. When they freed it of the earth and stones, they found it leaning down. The weight of the earth had caused it to slip from its position as a roofing stone. They pulled it free, and raised it out of the hole. It was a three-inch-thick flat slab that had been shaped, and when they lifted it out, the captain and George were standing on a passage floor that had been made from round rocks that had been sunk in the soil to make a sort of cobbled walk. The roof stone was not marked or decorated, nor was the flat stone on the other side of the passage. They were not long freeing the next roof stone, and when they had done so they stood in a passage that would have been about three feet square. Wherever it went, the men that built it would have had to crouch down to make their way through it.

"Agnes," the captain said. "We will rest now and eat."

"Later!" she said.

"Not later, now!" the captain said. "You hear me? Now. I'm tired. The boys are tired. Don't overwork a willing horse. We want to think about our next move. Come on, boy, up with you."

They had had to lower the rope ladder into the hole as it got deeper, so George came up and the captain followed him.

The woman stood there for a moment with her lips tight, and then she picked up the gun and stalked off toward the tent.

"I wonder where Babo is," Conor said.

It was the first time they had thought of Babo.

But when they got to the cell they found they needn't have worried about him.

He was sitting outside it with a half-loaf he had taken from the captain's tent and was picking mouseholes in it with his fingers.

They had to laugh at him.

"You know," said George, "that character is better able to look after himself than any of the rest of us."

"Here," said Edwin, "this old lady seems to be right about all this. We did come on the passage, didn't we?"

"I'll tell you," said George, "it's pretty exciting to be standing on stones that were put there so long ago. Don't you think so?"

"Yes," said Conor. "The look of the flat stone. It's in a geography book we do at school, all them circles on the stone. Isn't it funny to think that one of your own old people long ago sat down and did that stone."

"If the chamber is there," said Edwin. "Imagine breaking into the chamber! Imagine that, chaps!"

"Here," said Conor, "aren't we forgetting what kind of people they are and what they done to us?"

They thought of that.

"It doesn't matter now," said George airly. "We can think of that again when we get into the chamber. Imagine if that chamber is there and we get into it and nobody has been in it since it was closed. Imagine that!"

The captain came over to them. He sat down beside them on the grass. "Listen, boys," he said. "I've been thinking of the best thing for us to do next. If men are tunneling they dig a passage and block the sides and the roof with timber. Isn't that how it's done?"

"So?" said George.

"Well," said the captain. "Here we have a passage with the sides timbered, you might say, with stone. Now, if we clear a little above the area where the roof stone has fallen and push the roof stone back into position so that it rests again on the side stones, think of all the trouble we will have saved ourselves. Eh?"

They thought over it.

"That's it, Captain," said George. "You have a great idea there. The earth is well packed. I'm sure we can raise the roof stone without too much digging."

"That's it," said the captain. "We will go much faster."

He went away from them, back to the woman, who was cutting bread and opening canned meat.

"I wonder how far the tunnel goes?" Edwin said thoughtfully.

"Maybe it goes half a mile," said Conor. "How could we dig half a mile?"

"Anyhow, it's exciting, you know?" George asked. "It's exciting. Why doesn't the woman hurry up with the lunch?"

He had imitated the voice of the captain.

They laughed at him.

They could hardly understand themselves, but they were in a fever to get back to the passage. Edwin, the only one to give thought to it, began to understand a little how the Lady Agnes was feeling. She had been working and dreaming of this moment for such a long time. It was no wonder she was a bit dippy about it, if they themselves were so caught up with it.

They ate their lunch hurriedly and went back to the hole, their aches and blisters forgotten.

They watched anxiously as the captain cleared the earth from above the next fallen roof stone. The earth above was well packed and didn't fall. Then the captain raised the stone a few inches and scrunched his way in under it, got his enormous shoulders under it and raised it. He got it almost as high as the top of the side stone and when they cleared a little of the rubble from the top of it with the crowbar, he raised it another few inches, and the boys, digging in the crowbar at the side where it was resting on the side stone, pushed and pulled at it, until it slid across, very solidly, and formed a strong roof. They cheered when it went home. It hadn't taken very long.

The next one was more difficult because they had such a narrow space to work in. The captain had to come out so that the boys, with their smaller bodies, could get in and pass back the earth that had to be dug over the roof stone, but when that was done, the captain went back in and, using his great strength while Conor used the crowbar, he raised the second roof stone into position.

Then they heard him roaring.

"The passage is free!" he shouted, his voice muffled and magnified at the same time. "Listen, the next roof stones are in position. Get the lights! You hear? Tell her to go and get the lights."

She had heard him and was already running toward the cruiser.

The boys bent at the opening. The captain backed out toward them.

"Do you mean you don't have to dig anymore?" George asked.

"No," said the captain. "I could hardly believe it. I put in my arm and it was free to move. You see what has happened. The roof stones this far out had collapsed, but the pressure is not so great behind, so they seem to be in place. If this is so, all we have to do is go ahead and find the chamber."

"Can I go and see, Captain?" George asked.

"It's no use," said the captain. "You can't see without lights. Your body blocks most of the light that is coming from the hole we dug. We will have to wait for the lights. One of you go and get the lights from her. We'll have to see."

George went. He was the fleetest of them. He met the woman halfway to the cruiser and took a large flashlight from her and ran back with it, leapt into the hole, and handed it to the captain. The captain went back into the passage and George followed after him. The captain had to go almost pulling himself on his elbows, but George only had to bend and walk forward with his shoulders rubbing the roof. He could see the light illuminating the stones ahead of him. The passage went fairly straight. It was about twenty yards long. There were two curves in it, where the makers of the passageway might have been dodging huge boulders that they could neither remove nor cut through.

Then he heard the captain groaning. George looked over his shoulder. The light was shining on a solid block of rock. It must have been granite, because quartz crystals were reflecting the light back.

"It's like a dead end! A dead end!" he heard the captain say. "But no, wait a minute, the passage goes on to the left, and there is another roof stone fallen. Get the pickax and the crowbar. Hand them up."

George passed back the message and Edwin and Conor passed up the implements. George held the flashlight while the captain dug.

The Lady Agnes was now down at the mouth of the passage, calling, "Captain, what is it? What have you found?"

"Blocked, Agnes," the captain called back. "We are just blocked again."

He hacked away at the earth around the fallen stone and pulled it back with his arm. George pulled the loose earth to him then and passed it back to the others.

The captain was wet with sweat. His shirt was wet and his hair looked as if he had washed it. With his own strength he raised the roof stone, pushed it into place, and for a moment sat there, breathing heavily. Then he took the flashlight from George and shone it. There was a further length of passage. He went along this, and then the light shone on solid earth and stone that he knew from one look hadn't been disturbed in a million years.

"It's no good, no good!" he called. "We are in a false passage, a stinking false passage. This is the end."

There was a sound of despair in his voice.

chapter

13

It was amazing how the three of them were caught up in the thoughts of the digging.

Conor dreamed about it. He seemed to spend the whole of the night crouching in a passage that twisted and turned and went on and on endlessly. George and Edwin confessed that they had been dreaming about passages too, George's one being a nightmare. He was shut up in a tunnel and the air became harder and harder to breathe, so he was pleased to wake up and find that Babo's arm was across his mouth and there was no need to panic.

The captain called them.

They ate their breakfast, still finding it tasty, watching the furrowed brow of the captain as he thought and thought. "Did none of you get an idea in your head at all?" he asked.

"No," said George, "just that there must be a way

through. Why would they build an elaborate place like that if it was going nowhere?"

"Maybe something happened before they finished it," said Edwin. "Maybe they all died or something."

They watched the Lady Agnes emerging from the hole and coming down to them. Her hands were dirtied from the soil. She sat down. The captain handed her a cup of tea. She wasn't looking at them. She held the cup listlessly in her hands.

"I know there has to be a way," she said. "They didn't want it to be found. But it's there. Somewhere under our feet it is there, and we have to find it."

"If it's there," said the captain, "we'll find it."

Now the odd thing about it, Conor thought, is that I want to find it too. And he knew that the other boys felt the same. He wondered why this was. After all, these people had done them harm. They were being held on this island against their will; their parents must have gone through agony about them since the night of the storm, and yet here they were worrying about finding the Great Yellow Ox.

"There's something about that big stone," said George.

"What about it?" the captain asked.

"I don't know," said George. "Why is it there? Why is it just there?"

"They just came to it," said Edwin, "and had to stop going any farther. Do you think that is it, Captain?"

"I don't know," said the captain. "Let's go and have another look at that stone."

They went with him.

They all went down the ladder into the passage and crawled along it and focused the light on the great granite rock. There was room for all of them to sit and stare at it in the light of the flashlights because of the passage going to the left. It just seemed to be a solid block.

"Captain," said George, "let's see how far this stone goes."

"We'll soon find out," said the captain. He took a pickax and started to hack the side stone where it met the great rock. Since it was a flat limestone, it broke fairly easily down one side. Thus he uncovered the backing earth and the side of the big stone going into the earth. The boys moved the broken limestone and the earth behind them into the false passage.

The captain dug in a foot.

"There seems no end to it," he said. "No end."

"But there has to be an end," Edwin said. "Unless it is as big as the island."

Then there was a danger of the roof stone collapsing as the captain broke the side stone, so he had to stop and go back and bring down a piece of heavy timber to prop the roof stone. This took time.

While the captain was engaged in this, George kept hacking at the earth with the pick, and the boys scooped the loosened earth into the false passage.

Then George dug in a strong blow, and when he tried to withdraw the pick, he couldn't, so he got to his knees and levered and there was a crack and the handle of the pickax broke, leaving the pickax itself and about six inches of timber behind him. George fell on his back. He turned to them, waving the broken handle.

"Don't laugh," she said. "Just don't laugh, you guys."

"Wouldn't dream of it," said Edwin. "Ha. Ha. Ha."

"Jeepers, you looked funny," said Conor.

The captain came back with a heavy hammer. The prop he had put in was leaning out, so he hit it with the hammer and straightened it.

"What happened?" he asked then.

"I broke the pick," said George. "It's stuck in there."

"What is it stuck in?" the captain asked.

"That's right," said George. "What is it stuck in?"

The captain was already putting in his hand, digging out dirt, and feeling for the end of the pick.

"You found the end of the rock," said the captain. "That's where the pick is stuck."

"Now," said George, "what did I tell you?"

The captain tugged at the pick and freed it and threw it behind him and started to take away the rest of the soil with his hands. He took quite a pile of it away, which they moved, and then he shone a flashlight in the hole.

"What do you see, Captain?" George asked.

"I see the end of the rock," said the captain. "What good does that do us?"

"What's beyond the rock?" Edwin asked.

"Another rock," said the captain disgustedly.

"Do the rocks have straight edges?" Edwin asked. "I mean, are they regular edges or crooked?"

"What do you mean?" asked the captain.

"Well, if they are regular," said Edwin, "wouldn't you think that men had shaped them, but if they are all rough and crooked, maybe they were put there by nature."

The captain was looking at him, and put back his hand again and cleared the soil from the joint between the rocks.

"It seems a fairly regular joint," he said, "about half an inch wide. I can just get the tips of my fingers into it. It seems to be a straight joint."

"Wouldn't that mean," said Edwin, "that men joined them?"

"Maybe," said the captain, "but nature makes good joints too. It may be that the big rock just split like that. But there would be a passage here, and there is no sign of a passage."

They sat again and they looked at the rock. It was immovable, impassable.

They cleared the other side of it as well, by shifting the side stone and propping the roof stone, and they found the end of it, but it was just a rounded end sloping from bottom to top.

There seemed to be absolutely no way through. They sat there helplessly, looking at it.

The voice of Lady Agnes sounded from behind them.

"Well, Captain? Well, Captain?" She was down in the hole, peering at them through the opening.

"It's no use, Agnes," said the captain. "It's no use. There just seems to be no way through. I don't know what to do."

"There must be a way!" she cried. "There must be a way."

"There's no way, now," he said. "Come on, boys, we'll get into the air and eat a bit and think over it. Maybe something will strike us. It must be something simple. Damn it, they couldn't have come this far and then gone no further."

He set off.

They followed him.

Conor was the last, and as his hand fell on the pickax head he caught it and hit it against the great rock. It seemed to play a musical note, so he hit it again to confirm it, and then dropped the pickax and followed after the others.

When they got into the air, they found the sky was cloudless and the sun hot.

George said, "Captain, we want to go swimming."

Lady Agnes said, "No!"

The captain said sourly, "Why?"

"Because we are dirty," said George.

"All right," said the captain, "but no tricks." He was sitting in front of the tent. His arms were dirty from the earth-moving.

"Keep away from the boat," the lady said. "You hear that. Keep away from the boat. I will be watching."

She had picked up the shotgun again.

The boys turned off to the right to the rocky shore.

They stripped off their clothes there and went into the sea. Conor tracked down Babo first and had to do a lot of coaxing to get him into the water because he needed a wash as much as the rest of them, even if he hadn't been digging in tunnels. Conor washed him as well as he could with seaweed and sand and then let him go and swam about himself. He wasn't a very good swimmer. He could just do the breaststroke, but George was a good swimmer and so was Edwin.

Afterward they dried themselves on the rocks.

"These two are in a mess now," said George. "They have found nothing, so they will have to let us go."

"What will they say at home?" Conor asked.

"They will tell marvelous lies," said Edwin. "Grown-up people are great at telling lies because other grown-up people don't expect them to."

"Yeah," said George. "They'll say, 'What, those stupid kids, three boys and a half? You can't believe anything they say, always thinking up things that could never happen.' They won't believe us, you'll see."

"The captain and Lady Agnes look so respectable," said Edwin. "You'd never think they would tell a lie."

"How could we make up a thing like this?" said Conor. "They will have to believe us." He caught up a stone idly and flung it. It hit a standing stone near the water and skied off into the sea. He thought the sound of the two stones hitting was musical.

"It's a pity in a way," said George. "If we hadn't read all that about the god and things, it wouldn't have mattered; we'd have just thought the old lady was crazy and left it at that. But the story seemed as real as anything. And then we found the tunnel where they expected it and—"

"The stone was singing!" Conor shouted, suddenly sitting up.

"What?" asked Edwin, looking at Conor in amazement as he got up and started to get into his clothes.

"Are you nuts too, Conor?" George asked.

"No," said Conor. "Listen, I hit the rock with the pick and it sang a tune. You see. Come on. We'll tell the captain. That means the rock is hollow, you hear. All he has to do is to break the rock and see what's behind it."

He had his clothes on and was running up to the grass above them, calling, "Captain! Hey, Captain!"

The other two started to get into their clothes quickly.

"He's probably right," said George.

"I wish he hadn't said so," said Edwin.

"Why?" George asked.

"It would be better if they didn't get through to the treasure," said Edwin. "What's going to happen to us if they do find it?"

"It's too late now," said George.

And it was, because Conor was saying to the captain, "The stone sang when I hit it. It must be hollow. If you hit it with a hammer and break it, I bet you my life there's an opening behind it."

The captain ran and they followed him.

chapter

14

He was on his knees with the hammer poised in his hand. The rock looked as solid as ever.

"Listen," said Conor, hitting it with the broken pick.

Sure enough, the sound that came to them was not the sound of a solid rock.

The captain raised the heavy hammer and hit the rock.

The granite chipped under the blow, but it didn't break. All the same it didn't sound right. So this time he clenched the hammer hard and, drawing a deep breath, he hit it with all the power of his shoulders and the rock crumbled.

You could see that the broken pieces that fell were only inches thick.

"See! See!" said Conor.

"But there's another rock behind it," said the captain. "There's a space between them. That's what made the hollow sound."

He attacked the rock now with the hammer as if it were an enemy, his teeth clenched. Gradually it fell away from in front and bit by bit disclosed another rock behind. But this was not the same sort of rock. It was sort of oval, shaped like an egg.

They had been very clever with their rock cutting as they now saw. The big rock that looked square and solid had been chipped and cut so that it made a thin cover for the rock behind it, and this was fitting snugly into the hinder part of the rock. What patience it must have taken to scoop out all the thick rock just for the sake of making a slab to camouflage the oval one that obviously blocked the mouth of a further passage.

It was not long until they had all the granite chips out of the way and were looking closely at the oval rock.

The captain put up his hand and pushed at it. It made no move. It was firm and solid. He took up the hammer and hit it. It didn't sing. The hammer bounced off it.

"Why is it that shape?" Edwin asked.

"Maybe that was the way they found it," said George.

"No," said the captain, "there's a reason for the shape of it. Everything they did so far had a purpose in it. Why would they hide it if it wasn't the key to the chamber? Get me the crowbar."

Edwin got the crowbar.

He dug it in at the bottom and heaved. It made no move. He tried it again and again and again, until sweat was breaking out all over him, and it made no move.

Then he shifted the crowbar and inserted it near the

top and heaved and strained, but that was no good either.

He sat back, looking at it, his chest heaving.

"There has to be a way to get at it," he said.

"Maybe it swivels," said Edwin.

"What?" said the captain.

"Maybe that's why they have it that shape," said Edwin, "so that it swivels or something."

The captain kept looking at him for a few moments, then he put down the crowbar, spat on his hands, leaned close to the right side of the stone and pushed.

They were holding their breath.

The stone started to move from the strength of the captain's arms. It was just as Edwin had guessed. It was turning on a top and bottom axis. The boys put out their hands and pulled at the opening that was appearing. The rock swung toward them, showing a flattened inner surface, and inside a short, dark passage.

The captain flashed the light in it. This passage was only about six feet long, and the end of it was blocked by a square slab like the ones on the sides and the roof of the other passage. They could see in the light that it was highly decorated with Celtic carvings, like the early one they had seen.

The captain took the light and the hammer and went into the passage.

He examined it. He tapped it with the hammer. It rang hollow. He wondered if he would splinter it with the hammer. He had his hand raised to do so, when he paused. He really didn't like to break this slab with all its decorations. Not that it made any difference, considering all the damage he had done already. The captain had met a lot of ancient monuments men. He imagined what their anguish would be at the thought of the desecration of those beloved mounds of theirs, shrines that should be handled with care and delicacy.

Perhaps even this would not have stayed his hand, but then he saw a round hole on the left-hand side of the slab and another round hole on the right-hand side of the slab.

He put down the hammer and inserted his finger in one of the holes. You would think it was cut for his finger. He put the light under his chest and put a finger of his other hand into the other hole. He lifted and he felt the slab move.

He stopped then.

His pulses were pounding. He knew this was it. He knew that when he took away the slab that he would be able to enter into the chamber of Cathbadh and the Yellow Ox. He knew it just as well as if he had lifted the slab and shone the light in there.

He took away his hands from it and backed out.

"It's there," he told the boys. "All we have to do is to lift out one slab and we will be into the chamber."

"Go on and do it, Captain," George said. "Don't stop now. Let us see what's inside."

"Not yet," said the captain. "I don't know that I want to know what's inside. Suppose there is nothing at all, just a chamber, what is it going to do to my wife, Agnes? You read what she wrote about all this. Have you any idea what it all means to her? Do you know that it has become an obsession with her?"

"We know," said George grimly.

The captain sat with his back to the passage wall.

"Maybe what I should do is go and say we found nothing and let us all get to hell off this island," said the captain.

He thought this over.

It would be the right thing to do. They should just go away and tell the competent authority of their discovery, and let them take over, and handle the rest with care. She would win fame that way as the one who had set out and interpreted and finally tracked down this ancient monument with all that it might contain. She could spend the rest of her life writing authoritatively about it. No end to it in learned tomes and research magazines. She would be famous in these circles forever.

But he knew she wouldn't agree.

She alone had been right all along, and this entitled her to all the rights. This was the way she saw it. No other hand but hers. The captain sighed.

"I'll have to tell her," he said. "Don't do anything until I come back with her. Don't move. The last bit is for her. She must be the first person to go in there."

He crawled out of the passage, climbed the ladder into the open air, and walked slowly toward the bay and the cruiser.

The boys were silent.

"Now, maybe, we have a chance," said George.

"How do you mean?" asked Edwin.

"He goes down to the old lady," said George. "She comes running with the captain after her. In the meantime we are out of the hole and hidden and as they start running toward us, we run for the boat. Would it work?"

They thought it over.

Edwin said, "It might, maybe, but when they saw we were gone when they came back, the captain would be out of the hole like a rabbit and after us, and he would have the gun. He could pick us off at a hundred yards."

"We'd never see what's in there either," said Conor.

They thought this over.

"We worked hard enough to see what's in there," said George.

"It would be nice to see what's in there," said Edwin.

"So we don't run?" asked George.

They didn't answer him.

"Remember I made the plan for you, and you turned it down," said George. "If you had agreed to run, I would have thought up another plan to keep you here. I want to see what's in there as much as anyone. Hurry, Captain, hurry, hurry!"

"Maybe," said Edwin, "when the old lady gets what she wants she will become a different person."

They thought about that.

Conor remembered her eyes and he shivered.

"I hope so," he said fervently.

"After all," said George, "if it wasn't for us they couldn't have found this place."

That sounded good.

***

The captain stood on the rock and called at the boat, "Agnes! Agnes!"

He saw her come out of the cabin and stand in the cockpit.

"Well," she said, "still no success?"

He paused for a moment.

"We have found it, Agnes," he said.

He saw her face changing as if she had received a blow.

"You are sure?" she asked. "You are not just sounding a false alarm?"

"No," he said. "We have found it. There is just one slab between us and the chamber. I wouldn't move it until you came."

She stood looking at him a few minutes longer. She became pale, he saw, and her hands were clutching the sides of the boat. Then she loosened the rope tying the dinghy, stepped into the dinghy, and covered the few yards to the landing with her hands as paddles.

He helped her out of the dinghy, heaved it onto the shore, and took the shotgun from it.

"You are not fooling me?" she asked, her hand on his arm, squeezing it so much with her thin fingers that she was actually hurting him. "You are sure this is not another false alarm? I have had so much misfortune, I can't bear any more."

"The chamber is there," he said. "I swear it. There is nothing between you and the fulfillment of your dreams except a single slab of limestone."

She walked off toward the head.

He followed after her.

The strange thing, he thought, is that neither of them hurried. It was always the way. You want a thing badly enough to kill for it and then when you are ready to lay your hands on it, you wonder why you were so eager for it. He felt that way.

But she wouldn't.

She walked slowly because she was like a person in the desert walking toward water. She walked, he thought, almost reverently.

She went down the ladder.

He followed her.

"First I must see with my own eyes," she said.

The boys had pulled back into the false passage. She didn't even see them as she shone the light on the open oval rock and passage behind. The captain was close to her.

"You see," he said. "Look at the slab. You can see the finger holes for its removal."

"I must do that," she said. "Would I be able to do that?"

"Go in and try," he said. "I'll hold the light."

She went into the passage on her knees.

She put her fingers into the holes. She lifted and the slab came free.

"It's free," she said. "It's free!"

She put the slab to one side. "Now, give me the light," she said, "the chamber is here."

He handed her the flashlight and she shone its light into the chamber.

chapter

15

It was a round, squat chamber. The narrow stones were built one on top of another like the stones of the beehive cell up on the surface, but it was about three times the size.

The light of the flashlight showed all this as it swung around the walls.

But then it halted and stopped on a figure right opposite the opening.

You could see the light wavering as the hand of Lady Agnes shook. She moved into the chamber on her knees. She had to use her two hands to hold the light steady as she focused it. The captain had come in behind her, and he now had a flashlight too, which he shone. The boys crawled in behind the captain and peered from each side of him.

None of them in their hearts ever believed that it

would be there. None of them except Lady Agnes. But there is was. It was gleaming dully in the light, the Golden Ox, raised on two stone steps. It almost seemed as if it were alive. The massive head with its curved horns was lowered, one forefoot was raised as if to paw the ground, and the tail was curved as if it were going to lash. Magnificent muscles stood out from its body. Any moment they expected it to roar, paw the ground, and charge. It was truly magnificent, and somehow awe inspiring in the beams of the flashlights.

"You see! You see!" Lady Agnes said triumphantly, but she said it in a sort of whisper.

"Man! Man!" said the captain.

Lady Agnes moved forward, still on her knees. Her progress was halted abruptly by a big wide-mouthed urn that had been carved from rock, a sort of shallow saucer. She looked into this. There was a pile of ashes resting in it. She gripped the edges of the urn with her hand. "Look, Captain! Look, Captain!" she whispered. "There is what remains of Cathbadh the druid, just as I told you. There are the remains of the last pagan, his ashes resting in front of his god. I told you it would be this way."

"There's more," said the captain.

He had lowered his light, and now, beyond the urn, he illuminated a skeleton. The head of the skeleton was resting at the foot of one of two steps on which the ox was standing, and the feet were almost against the urn.

The Lady Agnes went around the other side of the urn and shone her light on the skeleton.

"Look!" she said. "Look!"

The skeleton was only about five feet long. The head was turned to the right. She reached her hand forward and lifted what had been around the neck. It was a necklace of rectangular plates about an inch wide joined by round bands. The plates were decorated with very fine lines, partly enameled. It was very delicate workmanship. She rubbed at the necklace with her palm, and the rings that joined the plates started to gleam. "Look," she said. "These are made of gold."

"There's more," said the captain. He reached his hand in between the bones of the breast and caught at what he could see. He raised it, holding it in his palm. It was a round circle band, blackened, about two inches across. He rubbed this too with his palm and it began to show colors.

"It's a brooch," she said. "It's a Celtic brooch. There should be a pin to go with it."

She took it from him and he put down his hand again and felt around and his fingers came up holding a pin about four inches long. The head of the pin was flat and had minute carvings on it. He rolled this pin between his fingers, and it began to gleam.

"I told you, Captain," she said, as he handed it to her. She took a large handkerchief from her pocket, placed it flat on the flagstones, and put the necklace and brooch into it.

"And more," she said, "and more." There was a bangle around what had been the ankle of the body and two on the wrist. The arm bones had separated. She took those. She could see there were minute carvings on the bangles.

The captain shone his light on the arms and legs of the skeleton on his side, and he saw three more. He picked them up and handed them to her.

The boys had been watching all this with the utmost fascination. It seemed a weird scene in the light of the flashlights, with the Yellow Ox menacing them from his height, the sight of the white-and-green-moldy bones of the skeleton, the gleaming eyes of the Lady Agnes as she peered at the treasures taken from the skeleton.

Fine, George, thought, but what are we doing here? She was right. There all those things are. What are we doing here? He knew what they should be doing. He pulled at Edwin's arm. Edwin was gazing, fascinated, at the scene in front of him. Conor was behind him. Now was the time, George tried to tell Edwin with his eyes. His mouth formed the word *run*. He could see it all. A quick scramble out of the chamber, push the oval stone into place, jam it with a piece of stone, and they could take their own time getting away. He wanted to kick himself now. When the Lady Agnes went into the chamber and the captain followed, that was the time for action. It was the attraction of the chamber that had made them lose their senses; the thirst to know what was in there, instead of using their heads to get away.

Edwin nodded, so George moved. He knew the other two were now aware and that they would follow.

Lady Agnes, for all her appearance of being mesmerized by the jewelry, saw George move.

She screamed "Captain! Captain!" and hurled herself back to the passage opening. She and George reached it together. She grabbed him about the shoulders with her hands. She screamed into his face, "You won't! You won't! You won't!"

"Stay still now! Stay quite still now!" the captain shouted. "Don't forget that I have the gun. Look at me and see it!"

George knew he had it. He had come down into the hole with the gun over his shoulder, the strap across his back. George stopped struggling. She would have been too much for him anyhow.

"Come back now," said the captain. "Let the three of you get close together there near the left side of the ox where I can keep an eye on you. Come on! Move fast! I won't tell you again!"

There was menace in his voice. They started to obey him. George was groaning as he moved over to the boys. One second, he thought. Just one more second and I would have been away. Even if he had gone himself, closed up Conor and Edwin with them, he could have gotten away and they couldn't have touched the others. They would just have had to wait there, sitting with their stinking treasures until they were released from the chamber. He sat with his head in his arms, feeling sick with himself.

Edwin patted his shoulder as if he knew. George looked up.

"Don't let there be a move out of you," said the captain. "I have said my last word on it."

"The little sneaks," said the Lady Agnes. "They would have ruined everything, everything."

She had put all the stuff carefully into the handkerchief. Now she rolled them in the handkerchief and put it into one of the big pockets of her tweed coat. Then she sat back on her heels and shone the light on the ox. It seemed to be looking directly at her. She went closer. She put out her hand and rested her fingers on the horn of the ox. It was about two and a half feet high, resting on a rectangular plinth of heavy metal.

"No wonder they worshiped you," she said. "No wonder they worshiped you. Have you ever seen anything like it, Captain?"

"No," said the captain. "I have never seen anything like it. It must be unique on the earth."

"And it's mine," she said.

"If that is the way you want it, it is yours," said the captain.

She got more daring. She put her hand on the head and the body of the ox.

"It's as if he were alive," she said. "Alive, as if you could feel it throbbing under your fingers. Wasn't I right, Captain? Wasn't it worth all the years, all the years?"

"You were right," said the captain. "It was worth it."

"Now we must get it out of here," she said. "Will you be able to carry it on your own?"

"I'll try," said the captain. "Hold the gun." He handed it to her.

"Listen," she said to the boys. "Don't move. I tell you, don't move."

The captain started to gather the bones of the skeleton.

"Was this a woman?" he asked.

"I think so," she said.

"How did she die?" he asked her.

"She died for the god," said Lady Agnes, "when Cathbadh was cremated and his ashes put in the urn."

"You mean they killed her?" he asked.

"What does it matter?" she asked. "She had a good end, better than most of us."

The captain put the bones in on top of the ashes in the urn. "Well, she and the druid can be together for always now," he said. He got to his feet. He could stand in the chamber. The roof, before it started its curving slope, was about a foot over his head. He stood in front of the ox. He put an arm under the head of the ox and under the body and lifted. The ox came with him. He almost staggered under its weight.

"It's heavy," he said.

"What do you expect?" she asked. "It's solid gold."

He rested the plinth on his knee and got a better grip on the ox. Then he walked with it to the opening out of the chamber. He put it on the flag there and got in front of it and backed out, pulling it toward him.

"Be careful with it, Captain." she called. "Be tender with it."

"I'll be careful," he said. He backed out carefully, hauling it after him. It rode well on the flags.

She followed him up, facing the boys. The captain had left his flashlight on the ground behind him. She left it there. When she came to the opening she got to her knees and backed out into the passage, the gun pointing back at the boys, the light blinding them.

The captain was waiting near the oval stone.

"Now what?" he asked.

"Close them in," she said, "until we get time to organize ourselves. We want to get these things to the boat first, and we cannot be fretting about what they will do. We can come back again."

"Right," said the captain.

He used his strength to close the oval stone on the opening. Then, just to make sure, he got a chunk of the broken granite and, using his heavy hammer, he jammed it under the stone.

"There," he said, "that will keep them safe until we are ready to talk to them again."

"It's so beautiful, so beautiful, so beautiful," she was saying, on her knees staring at the ox.

"But it's only a statue," said the captain. "A very valuable statue, but still it's only a statue."

"No!" she said. "It is more! It is much, much more. Let us get it down to the boat and we can have a real look at it."

They maneuvered the heavy statue toward the hole in the hill. There they raised it out of the ground into the late afternoon light with the block and tackle. There the captain made two loops of rope and canvas and slung the heavy weight of it on his back and they set off toward the boat.

Down below, Edwin switched off the flashlight. "We might need it," he said. In the darkness George spoke. "Now, where are we?" he asked, and they couldn't answer him.

chapter
16

They had some trouble getting aboard the cruiser with the load. But the captain was a strong man, and finally the treasure was on the table in the cabin, lighted by the eerie glow of the declining sun through the portholes and the skylight. The captain was exhausted. He had to sit.

Lady Agnes leaned on the table, looking into the baleful eyes of the Yellow Ox. They seemed baleful to the captain because of the way the light was falling on the figure. For a few moments he was apprehensive, wondering whether they should have left this thing where it had been, where it had been undisturbed for so long. Maybe they were wrong to bring it into the light.

He shrugged off these fancies. It was only a lump of gold. Even if it was melted down it would be worth a very handsome amount. As it stood he knew that it was priceless. Why should a thing like that be left buried in a dark chamber?

"Go now," she said to him, not taking her eyes off the ox, "and take food and drink to those boys. Collect the small one on your way and put him down there with them."

The captain stirred uneasily.

"Is that a place for a small fellow?" he asked. "Won't it frighten him?"

"He'll be more frightened on his own," she said. "Go and do that and I will be up later."

The captain pulled at his lower lip with his fingers.

"What will you do about the boys?" he asked.

"You leave the boys to me," she said. "They will be all right. Just do what I tell you."

"After all, if it wasn't for them we wouldn't have found that chamber so fast," he suggested.

Now she looked at him. Her eyes were blazing.

"We would have come on that chamber," she said, "if I had to excavate every inch of it with my fingernails. You hear? Those boys were nothing but trouble and worry. From the very first. They rushed us into all this. They upset all my plans. We could have come and gone at our leisure and nobody would ever have known, ever. Go and do what I told you, Captain."

He shrugged his shoulders, lifted a protesting hand, and let it fall again. He rose and went out of the cabin. After all, it was her affair. She was his boss. As he got on the dinghy, went to the shore, and started to walk to the tent, he thought of this. He had been more than fond of the drink before he married her. And when a man drinks, a wife must take over and run things, since the man neglects everything but the drink. He didn't drink as much now, but her ascendancy remained, he thought ruefully. Thought of drink brought him to the tent. He went in and sat on the cot with the sleeping bag and he opened a bottle and he drank deeply from it.

Satisfied, he rose and came into the open again. He looked at the sky. In the east the clouds low at the horizon were beginning to take on a tinge of color. He knew there were about two hours until darkness.

He went around the back of the cell, and there he saw Babo, busily engaged in gouging handfuls from a loaf. He had practically excavated it, until only the crust remained.

He stopped eating. His eyes became frightened when he saw the captain. The captain was afraid that he was going to get up and run away. He had an unpleasant picture of himself chasing the little fellow and carrying him, struggling and screaming, down below.

"Do you know where your brother is?" he asked softly.

Babo looked at him very warily and shook his head.

The captain squatted.

"Well, I do," he said. "You saw us digging the hole. Well, there is a lovely cave down there like you read about in storybooks. Your brother and the lads are there, and I want to bring them down food and water, as they are busy digging. I was wondering if you would help me."

Babo listened to this closely, and then he nodded.

How low can you go? the captain wondered, looking into the innocent blue eyes.

"Right," he said, rising. "Come on and help me. You can bring that piece of a loaf with you."

He walked away from him, wondering if he would follow. He went to the tent. He got one of the buckets and went to the place near the old church where there was a spring. He filled the bucket with water. Then he went back to the tent and got a small sack and put bread and butter and canned stuff into the sack, as well as a can opener and a knife. He handed Babo a can of condensed milk.

"You carry that," he said and walked toward the hole, thinking that everything would be all right. His stomach was warm from the drink. Things looked better. They had achieved something wonderful. It was nearly equal to climbing Mount Everest, or discovering the North Pole, or voyaging to the moon. He chuckled at this thought. But it was a wonderful achievement. It was a pity they couldn't tell the whole world about it.

He went down the hole carefully with the bucket and the sack. He left them then and helped Babo down the rope ladder. Babo was quite interested in going down the hole.

"Now," he said to Babo, "you just wait here until I come back for you." There was a wire handle on the flashlight. He put this in his teeth when he switched on the light and made his way to the oval stone. Then he shone the light back and called, "You come now, little fellow." Babo came walking upright, he was so small. He was looking around him with wonder, clutching his scooped-out loaf and his can.

"Now," said the captain, "you give me the can and hold the light."

Babo was pleased to do this too.

The captain found the hammer and hit out the stone wedge and pressed on the stone until it opened.

"Now," he said, "you go on in there and you will find your brother."

Babo was a bit doubtful, but he went in a few steps and called, "Conor! Conor!" and when he heard the voice of his brother calling, "Babo, here I am, Babo!" he ran through the short passage and Conor was waiting there for him and took him into his arms. George had switched on their own light.

Now the captain followed Babo, with the bucket and the sack.

"What did you bring Babo for?" Conor asked indignantly.

"He wanted to be with his brother," said the captain smoothly. "Now, here you are. Food and drink for you."

"Why can't you let us go above to the cell?" Edwin asked.

"Aren't you far safer down here?" the captain asked, chuckling. "When you are down here in this nice cozy place, we know we can sleep easily without having our sleep interrupted. We will be leaving tomorrow morning, and we will free you before we go. Are you hungry?"

Of course they were hungry, as he well knew. "I will leave you the food and the second flashlight," he said. "Sleep well."

He was gone then, and they heard him closing the

stone and driving the wedge. They looked at one another, but they had to be cheerful since Babo was looking at them.

"Well," said George, "let's get eating. Tomorrow is another day."

"Isn't this a grand, funny place to be, Babo?" Conor asked him. Babo was looking around him. He didn't think it was funny. One small hand was clutching Conor's arm.

"Like a story, Babo," said Edwin. "Just like a story your mother would tell you."

He didn't know if this cheered Babo up, but they were hungry and they started to set out the things to eat.

When the captain climbed out of the hole, she was there waiting, sitting on a rock.

"Well?" she asked.

"They are all there now," he said.

"Good," she said. "Now we will fill in the hole."

He was staggered.

"What did you say?" he asked.

"We will fill in the hole," she said.

"We can't do that," he said. "How will we let them out in the morning?"

"We are not letting them out in the morning," she said.

"But we have to let them out in the morning," he shouted.

"Are you going mad?" she asked. "We must have time. In the morning we will leave here and pack up. Then we will set out for the place in Cornwall. The weather reports are good. We can easily be around the coast and down into Cornwall in two or three days. Then, when we have everything ready, we can make a phone call. It is as simple as that. They can dig the hole, find the passage and the boys, and they will never find us after that. It's simple."

"They won't have any air down there," the captain said. "They'll smother to death."

"There's plenty of air down there," she said. "There's more than enough for them for a few days. What's come over you, Captain? Are your going to ruin everything now, at this last minute, in the midst of this triumph?"

"No, but three days down there will drive them mad."

"What?" she said. "Are you an idiot? It might drive intelligent people mad, but not those dreadful little extroverts. Captain, come to your senses. It's the only thing to do. We cannot leave them running loose around the island. They would find some way to communicate with the shore. Think of them. The things they have done already. This is the only way to keep them quiet and safe until we ourselves are safe. Cannot you see this, Captain?"

She had her hand on his arm, looking into his eyes.

"Yes," said the captain reluctantly. "I suppose so. And you swear that we will make that phone call?"

"Captain," she said, "what is your opinion of me? Am I a monster? Would I kill four children for the sake of all this?"

The captain looked at her. He was a bit bewildered. Everything she said seemed to make sense, and yet, when he thought of the dedicated years in which she had pursued her goal, he wondered. But she couldn't be like that. She wouldn't hurt a fly, hurt a fly, hurt a fly, he hoped.

"All right," he said, "if you think this is the best thing to do."

He climbed into the hole again. He went along the passage and collected the tools—the hammer, the other pickax, the crowbar, and the shovels—and he threw them out. Then he climbed out of the hole for the last time and drew up the rope ladder after him.

He paused there again then.

"You are sure now, Agnes?" he asked. "You are sure?"

"Captain," she said. "Have you no faith in me? Haven't I led you successfully until now? Haven't things turned out the way I said they would?"

"That's right, Agnes," he said, "that's right." And he spat on his hands and started throwing the big rocks down into the hole. She herself took up a shovel and started throwing the earth in, like filling in a grave, the captain thought, and shivered, and put the thought out of his head. It would take them an hour to fill in the hole, and put back the sod, but that was much less time than it had taken to dig the hole. He cleared his mind of uneasy thoughts then and got down to the job.

***

The boys were eating sandwiches by flashlight when they heard the thump, thump, thump. The sound came clearly in to them, magnified in fact by the passages.

They looked at one another. They listened. They didn't want to believe their ears, but there could be only one conclusion to be drawn from the sounds. The hole was being filled in, and the four of them were being more or less buried alive in this chamber of the dead.

They lost their appetites. The three elder boys felt panic in their stomachs, but they just had to sit, stiff and terror-stricken, in the chamber under the ground.

chapter

17

George switched off his flashlight, and Edwin the one near to him. It was an instinctive gesture on their part, as if they wanted the dark to hide their feelings.

Babo said, "Why is it dark, Conor?"

Conor said, "Shh!"

They listened to the thumping for some time and then gradually it became more muffled until they couldn't hear it anymore.

Conor felt terrified. It wasn't just the darkness, because he knew they could brighten the darkness. It was a feeling of suffocation.

It reminded him of once when they were in the hayfields, playing with a new stack of hay, which they shouldn't have been doing, the top of it collapsed and he was underneath and was smothered in the fall of the hay.

He remembered the feeling of panic, the moments when he could do nothing and then starting to tear frantically at the hay that covered him, trying to find air and light. The others were pulling the hay away from him from the outside, but it seemed like a whole lifetime before his face was freed and he could see the sky and breathe again.

Edwin was trembling. He couldn't stop it. It might be the accumulation of all the things that had happened to them in a few days, which seemed like a dream, until now. The thumping seemed to put the seal of truth on it all, and there was nobody to come to their rescue, no mother, no father, no big brother or sister. He remembered being closed up too, in a dark closet under the stairs, when they were playing hide-and-seek, and he had gone in there, forgetting that the closet could be opened only from the outside. The smell of floor polish and polish-soaked cloths came to him now as he remembered banging and kicking at the cupboard door, screaming at times. It was a long time before they heard him, because they thought he had gone out of the house. He still remembered the joy and overwhelming relief of seeing the light when they opened the door. Ever since, when he was frightened, he smelled floor polish, and he was smelling it now.

George was overwhelmed with the feeling of being very young. Nothing like this had ever happened to him before. Nobody had ever been unkind to him. His father left his upbringing to his mother and she would spend hours reasoning with him. He had never even come across bad people, except in watching films or television or reading books, but he knew that was unreal, even if he could be frightened while watching or reading. But this was real. It came over him in a flood of fear that they were being harmed and they had done nothing to deserve it. Nobody had ever been in such a position as they were now. He started to shake. He knew this reaction was bad, so to overcome it he talked.

"You know something," he said, having to cough to clear his throat and wondering at the shakiness of his voice. "I'm glad they took that ox out of here."

They listened to him. They found it hard to speak.

Conor said, "Why?"

"I don't know," said George. "Didn't like the look of the thing. Did you, Conor?"

"No," said Conor. "It was well made, but it made me afraid."

They listened to that word *afraid* and it did something for them. It was at least spoken out loud, and when they heard it, it didn't seem so bad.

"I don't mind the skeleton so much," said George. "Do you mind the skeleton, Edwin?"

"No," said Edwin shakily, "that's all right, just that it was probably a young one like ourselves that didn't want to be here no more than we do."

"Or the ashes of Cathbadh," said George airily. "I don't mind him. He was a good old guy. He just believed in things and went ahead with what he thought was best."

150

"Old Cathbadh was all right," said Edwin.

"I bet old Cathbadh wouldn't do a thing like this," said George, "to a few kids who never did anything to him."

"Is Babo listening, Conor?" Edwin asked.

"Are you all right, Babo?" Conor asked. As soon as the darkness came Babo had climbed on top of Conor and had an arm wrapped around his neck.

"Yes," said Babo. "Why is it dark?"

"There," said George, switching on the flashlight, "it's not dark anymore."

He allowed the beam of the flashlight to shine on Conor and the boy. They looked at the baby face. George swiftly took the light away from him. They saw the tears on his face.

George felt like cursing. Imagine doing a thing like this to a little baby, he fumed. The sight of Babo had made Edwin's panic flee before a feeling of anger.

He switched on his light too and circled the chamber with its beam, all around it and the roof. As it flashed past the roof, something caught his attention and he flicked back the light there again, but it wasn't anything much, so he shone the light on the passage.

"It's a pity we're not rabbits," he said.

"We'd need to be rabbits with steel claws," George said.

He suddenly went into the passage and when he reached the oval stone he banged and pushed at it.

"It's no use," he said, coming back. "He has it wedged from outside. That's what I would do myself. You know what? We ought to finish eating. Are you hungry, Conor?"

"I am indeed," said Conor, who wasn't in the least hungry.

"Me too," said Edwin, who wasn't either, but it would be doing something, wouldn't it, taking their minds off their predicament?

George doused his light and Edwin put the other one on the ground and they took up their meal where they had left off. Even Babo was induced to eat, but he wouldn't leave his place on Conor's lap. Edwin still remembered the tears on his cheeks, shining in the rays of the flashlight, and he was surprised at his own anger.

"You know," he said. "Babo is very good. If that was another kid he'd be screaming the place down."

Conor felt that too. "He's all right," he said.

"Listen," said George, "if it wasn't for Babo, this expedition would have been a complete failure."

"And what is it now?" Conor asked.

They thought over his question and suddenly it seemed funny. George laughed.

"That's right," he said. "What is it now indeed? Was there ever anybody else in the predicament that we are in now?"

Suddenly Edwin got to his feet and shone the light on the roof over their heads. He had suddenly remembered what he had seen. He had seen Babo's tears and when he had changed the light, he had seen something on the roof that reminded him of the tears. He saw it again now, a blob of water reflecting the light. It was coming from an area of the roof where the big capping stone was resting on the others. On the right side of it there was a green area about a yard wide, and it was at the center of this green area that he had seen the blob of water that resembled the tears of the child.

"Listen," he said. His voice was tense.

"What is it, Edwin?" George asked.

"Come over here, George," he said. "You are taller than me. Reach up to that green patch there in the roof, all that moss around the stones, and pull at the stones with your fingers."

George got to his feet and went over. He reached up to the middle of the green patch and pulled at one of the overlapping stones with his fingers and it came away in his hand.

"It's rotten, the stone," he said. "It's soft and crumbly."

Now Edwin was trembling again, but he was trembling with excitement.

"Look," he said, sitting down again. "Let us think."

"What do we think about?" George asked.

"We think about that hole we dug," said Edwin. "Remember. How deep was that hole before we came to the passage?"

"The hole itself was about eight feet to the slab stones," said Conor.

"And the passage was about three feet," said Edwin. "That makes eleven feet. How high is this chamber from the floor to the roof?"

George stood up and put up his hand.

"It's about seven feet at its highest," he said, puzzled.

"Well," said Edwin with great excitement in his voice, "that means that there are only four feet of dirt over us if we could make a hole in the roof."

They thought about this.

"Four feet," said Conor.

"Maybe a foot or two more if there's a hill but that's all there can be," said Edwin. He stood up and shone his light again on the green patch. "Look, the water has been seeping there for centuries. It has rotted the stones on that side. It we could get enough of them out, the big capstone might fall and then there would be only soil between us and the air." He was very excited. His voice squeaked on some of the words.

"He's right, you know. He's right," said George. He was pulling at the stones with his fingers. The edges of them came away. Where they broke they were rust-colored.

"See," said Edwin. "See!"

"Yeah, I see," said George, "but we will only get a few inches of them away with our fingers."

"Would a pickax be any help?" Conor asked, himself now excited.

"What do you mean a pickax?" George asked scornfully. "Do you think we go around with pickaxes in our pockets?"

Conor put Babo on his feet.

"Shine the light here," he said.

They did so, both of them.

"Look," he said, holding up the pickax with the broken handle.

"No," said George. "I don't believe it! Where did you get it?"

"I was tapping the stone outside with it, you remember," said he. "And when we all came in to see what was in the chamber, I had it in my hand, and forgot it."

George put his hand on his shoulder.

"A genius," he said. "A pure genius." Then he took it from his hand and went back and started hacking at the stones covered with the green patch. They started to fall, but George had to stop.

"It's no good," he said, "it's too high for me to reach. We need something to stand on."

"The best thing to do is to turn the big urn upside down," said Edwin. "That way it will preserve what's in it in case we manage to knock the roof in. Come on."

The three of them went to the right of the urn, leaving the flashlights lying on the ground. It required all their strength, but they turned it over so that its gaping mouth was down. They felt funny handling it, knowing what was in it: the bones of the skeleton and the ashes of the dead druid.

"It's in a good cause," said George, as if to ease the uneasiness they were feeling.

He stood now on the upturned bottom of the urn and his head was close to the roof so he could hack away at the stones. He had to use both hands, because the broken handle was so short.

The stones came away in showers now, broken into small pieces by the action of the seeping water. They were rotten a long way in. Conor relieved George and Edwin relieved Conor. The capping stone was enormous, a great granite one. It seemed to have no end, but everything has to have an end and they found an end to it about two feet inside.

There came a time when they could see that the end of the stone was resting only on two pieces of healthy rock. And then they had to be careful, because it would fall, and if it fell on one of them it would kill. So George gently tapped at the two edges that held it, and then when he saw movement, he jumped down and pulled back. They watched the big stone slowly detach itself, reluctantly. The end came free and then, painfully it seemed, it extracted itself from the earth to which it had been pressed for so long and fell slowly and gracefully into the chamber below. It fell on its end and then toppled backward as they watched it, holding their breath. It fell flat and missed the edge of the urn by a bare half-inch. Otherwise it would have broken it in pieces.

"Now," said George, letting his breath go.

He stood on the rock and examined the soil that had remained fixed. He hit at it tentatively with the pick, and it started to cascade. He hit it another blow, and then got down and ran. Tons of dirt fell, covering the big rock, spreading over the urn and the ground, making a big mound.

They looked at one another when it had ceased to fall.

They were very joyful. They knew now that they were going to get out of that chamber. Against all the odds they were going to get out. Nobody could have believed it possible, but they were going to get out of it.

George went up the mount and examined the hole with the flashlight.

"Listen," he said, "there's nothing up there now but a flat slab. I can see it. But it's too high. Both of you stand on the mound and I'll get up on your shoulders."

They did so. They bent their backs and he climbed on them, holding to the roof with his hands. Then they straightened themselves, and George found his head right under the flag. He put his palms under it and pushed and it stuck for a little while and then he had the whole weight of it, so he pressed upward and sidled it sideways, and he felt fresh air on his face.

For some reason, he whispered.

"I'm going up to see what's there." He caught the edges with his hands and raised himself up. They felt his weight gone from their shoulders and they straightened thankfully.

They waited tensely.

"Put out the lights," they heard him whispering. They did so.

"You won't believe this," they heard him say. He was leaning down into the chamber. "That slab was on the floor of the beehive cell. You hear? The cell was built right over the chamber. I have looked out. The captain is in the tent. There is a light in there. Boy, is that captain in for a surprise. Easy now."

chapter
18

They handed Babo up to George.

The amazing thing about it was that when they went to look for him he was curled up in a ball where Conor had left him before they started hacking, and he was fast asleep with a piece of bread still clutched in his hand.

"Aren't kids amazing?" said Edwin as if he were a hundred years old himself.

"Isn't it a great thing for him?" said Conor.

He barely woke up when George took him.

"Everything is fine now, Babo," he whispered to him, but Babo's eyes closed again, so he placed him on the floor, where he promptly went to sleep again. George was sorry that he had nothing for him to lie on or anything to cover him with, but the cell had been cleared of the bed of bracken they had put in it. This seemed very sinister to George, as if their captors wanted to wipe out every sign of them.

Edwin emerged from the chamber, and both of them pulled Conor out of it and then they replaced the slab, and, lying on their stomachs, peeped at the tent, which was only a few feet away from them. The flaps were closed and the light illuminated the white canvas.

"What do we do now?" Edwin whispered.

They had been quite a long time getting out of the chamber. Already there was a white streak low down on the sky in the east. The dawn couldn't be more than two hours away.

"Stay here," said George. "I'll go and have a look at things." He crawled out of the opening on his stomach, went to the left of the tent, and was soon out of their sight.

Actually he needn't have worried, because the captain was fast asleep, and he was in a very deep sleep.

When he had slapped down the last of the pieces of sod with the shovel, he had carried most of the tools and the equipment to the cruiser. Even if they had wanted to leave the island then, it was too late because darkness was falling, and there was no way to negotiate the rocky and dangerous bay except in the light of day. They could walk to the cruiser because the tide was out, and he stowed the gear and came away, leaving the Lady Agnes in the lopsided cabin admiring the Yellow Ox and starting to clean the ancient jewelry with a fine brush and cloth.

The captain was depressed.

He walked back to where the hole had been and he stood for a long time looking at it. The thought of the boys down there was not at all comforting to him.

He went into the tent, lit the mantle of the gas lamp hooked to the bottled gas outside, and sat heavily on the cot.

He was very uneasy. He got a bottle from his chest and filled a glass and drank it. He waited for it to cloud his mind so that he would not be thinking so clearly.

It seemed to take a long time.

He thought of Agnes, bending over their treasures in the lopsided cabin, with the polished and gleaming ox looking at her, and he shivered. She seemed to have divorced herself even from him. He had to make up his mind that she was a different person.

They had met when he was the captain on a cruise liner. He was on his last cruise as captain, but she didn't know that. The company was easing him out. She didn't know that. Because he was weak, the captain thought, hitting his knee with a clenched fist.

She was a nice person then. She had a sense of humor. She dressed well and she looked like a lady. Once or twice when they had landed at strange places he had gone with her while she dug up things with her little shovel. He had tried hard to be sober all those times and had succeeded, and he had known she would be good for him. She lived in Cornwall and had a little money, and that with his pension would set them up nicely.

If only they hadn't gone to live in his broken-down place, the last inheritance of the Maelrua, they would never have reached the stage they were at now.

She wasn't the same person at all.

He took another glassful of whiskey.

He liked those boys, that was his trouble. The things they had done, the efforts they had made to feed themselves, to try to escape the situation they were in had aroused his admiration. He was fond of kids. He always liked the kids who were on the cruises with their parents.

And that little blond fellow buried in a hole in the ground? That was not good. He could imagine him down there, screaming and crying with desperation and panic. He didn't like to think of this at all.

Would she make that phone call?

That was what was troubling him.

All right, they wouldn't die for three days down there. There was enough air for them, enough food, and light from the flashlights if they went easy with the batteries. All right, that was fine, but when the time came, would she make that phone call? If she didn't (not that he didn't think for a minute she wouldn't), but if she didn't and those four died, wouldn't it be murder? It would be something he would have to live with for the rest of his life. Would the Yellow Ox and the ancient ornaments be sufficient compensation? He didn't think they would.

He got another drink.

Things didn't seem to be so bad after that. He could trust Agnes, he thought. If she said she was going to make a phone call, then she would make a phone call. By that time, he was sure, nobody would be able to trace them or the Yellow Ox. She was a great one for phoning. Of course if she didn't phone then nobody would ever know about the Yellow Ox at all, and that was what worried him. It would be such a temptation not to make that phone call, just to let things slide, and if she did that would he be strong enough to make her do so?

He groaned and he had another drink, and then he took off his boots and his trousers and he struggled into the sleeping bag on the folding cot, and he poured himself another drink. Just one more, he thought, and I will go to sleep and all these thoughts will be blotted out.

Before he fell asleep there was something nagging at his mind. Something he ought to have taken note of. Something he had taken note of but had forgotten. What was it? He tried to remember, made a good effort to remember, but fell off to sleep. He didn't put out the light. He was a grown man, and he wasn't afraid of the dark, but the dark would remind him of the place below, where the boys were, so that was why he didn't put out the light.

When George cleared the tent, he got to his feet and walked fast toward the cruiser.

He went to the shore and came up to the rock that sheltered the bay from there. The tide was coming in and the cruiser was floating. There was a light in the cabin of the cruiser. He went out on the rock as far as he could go to try to see. He got an oblique look and could see the Lady Agnes in the cabin, sitting at the table, using her arms on something before her.

When he saw this, he drew away again and went back toward the tent.

He wondered why the light was still on.

He stopped at the back of the tent. It was held down by metal pegs. He gradually, slowly, slowly, pulled out the one at the corner and the one in the middle, and he raised the canvas gently until he could put the side of his face on the grass and look into the lighted interior.

He saw the captain, fast asleep. He was on his back. He wasn't snoring, just blowing out through his thick lips. His arms, those powerful arms, were tucked into the sleeping bag.

He let the canvas fall and thought awhile.

We will have to immobilize the captain, he thought. That is the first thing. Then we can take care of the woman. How do you put a huge, strong man out of action? he wondered. He was in a deep sleep. He knew this more from the sight of the half-empty bottle and the glass than from the sight of the captain.

Remembering the cot, he thought of a way that might be dangerous but that might also work.

He would have to discuss it with the others, but in the meantime he searched around outside the tent by the light filtering from it, and he came on the length of rope, neatly coiled, as befitted a sailor. He took this coil of rope and he crawled back into the cell.

"Well? Well?" Edwin whispered.

"Come close with your heads," said George. They put their faces very close to his.

"Do you remember *Gulliver's Travels*?" he asked.

"What part?" asked Edwin.

"When he was wrecked in Lilliput," said George. "When he woke up, what did he find?"

"He was bound down with hundreds of little ropes," said Conor. "His hair and all. I remember that."

"The little people did that," said George. "Well, we are little people and the captain is very big, so suppose we crawl in there with two ropes and tie him down on the cot. Isn't it the same thing?"

They thought about it.

"It is," said Edwin. "How do we do it?"

"There are legs on the cot," said George. "The captain is on top of the cot in a sleeping bag. We crawl in there. Conor has one rope. He puts it under the cot, brings it over the bag, and ties it tight, fast. That's his legs taken care of. You and I, Edwin, go one each side of the cot, and tie the rope tight and fast about his arms. His arms are in the bag. If the knot is good and tight, as it should be with two of us pulling at it, that should hold him until we get down to the boat."

"It sounds good, if we can do it," said Edwin.

"We have to do it," said Conor.

"What do we do then?" Edwin asked.

"We go to the boat and entice the woman out of there," said George. "You three can hide behind the rock. I'll shout things at her. She will follow me. You get on the boat. You know how to run one of these boats, Edwin?"

"I do," he said. "But where are you?"

"I'm chasing around the island," said George, "and she's after me."

"With a shotgun," said Conor. "We won't go unless you come with us."

"I will be with you," said George. "I swear. This is the only way it will work. You cut the ropes and back out of here and take the boat around to the head where we started digging. I'll join you from there."

"Are you sure?" Edwin asked.

"You'll see," said George. "And even if I don't, what can they do if you have gotten away? They just have to sit around here, waiting to be picked up while I tell them funny stories from *Joke Magazine*."

They thought it over.

"It sounds good," said Edwin. "Let's hope it will work."

"It will have to work," said Conor. "We will have to make it work. Aren't they awful people to close us up like that? Did they want us to die, do you think?"

"I think so," said Edwin. "We were the only evidence. They mightn't have wanted to, but they would have done it."

"We'll have to wait for the light," said George. "Say another hour, then we will have to move. If this doesn't work, I'm going to try and swim away to the shore."

"It's ten miles," said Conor. "There are fierce currents like the captain said."

"I don't care," said George. "But I won't have to. All we can do now is wait. Here, Conor, get your little knife and cut off two lengths of this rope."

Conor cut the rope, and then they lay on the ground watching the dawn gradually capturing the eastern sky.

chapter
19

It was a cold-looking dawn, faintly warmed by the yellow band of light being pushed ahead of it by the rising sun.

"Now," said George, and they squirmed out of the cell, pulling themselves forward with their elbows and bodies like young eels. George and Edwin went one to each side and Conor approached the closed flaps of the tent.

He paused to give them time to pull out the pegs on their sides and then he put his hand in through and opened the tied flaps inside. When they were free, he took a deep breath, tried to calm the pounding of his heart with a deep swallow, and then he eased himself into the tent.

It looked odd with the dawn light outside fighting the artificial light inside. He had the rope in his hands. The crossed legs of the bottom of the folding cot were facing him. He put one end of the rope under the cot and then rose to his knees with an end of the rope in each hand ready to pull it over the bottom part of the sleeping bag. He waited.

He saw George on his left and Edwin on his right, creeping under the canvas. George had the rope. He pushed one end under the cot and Edwin caught it. Then they both rose to their knees, holding an end of the rope.

George made a signal and the three of them rose to their feet.

Conor's heart was pounding so hard he thought it would choke him. The captain seemed to be in a deep sleep. He was lying on his back, breathing heavily.

They were both watching George.

He said, *Now!* with his mouth, and they went into action with trembling hands.

Conor made a quick knot as tightly as he could across the end of the bag. When he had the knot made, he tightened it and made another knot and pulled again. As soon as he had that done, without waiting for anything else, he went out of the tent and back into the cell and bent over Babo. "Babo!" he called. "Wake up! Wake up! We have to go!" He had to shake him, but he wasn't fully awake. He put out his arms and Conor scooped him up. "We have to go to the boat, Babo," he said, "but you must be quiet. Please be quiet. Don't make a sound."

Babo grabbed him more tightly and buried his face in his shoulder, so Conor went out of the cell and waited at the tent. He was waiting to hear the roaring of the captain.

So were George and Edwin.

They pulled the first knot tight just below the captain's shoulders. They tightened it by putting a foot against the side of the cot to give more strength to their pulling. And then they quickly tied another knot. George put his hand on the first one, while Edwin formed the second, and then they pulled again.

They didn't wait for anything else.

They went out of the tent as fast as they could.

As he left, George just saw the eyes of the captain opening, and as he saw a look of bewilderment coming into them, he joined the others outside and they ran toward the cruiser in the bay.

They didn't talk. Their hearts were in their mouths anyhow, so it would have been difficult for them to talk. But they knew what they had to do.

They went left and got onto the shore in order to come up on the big rock beside the cruiser. It wasn't easy to travel the shore now and keep their heads down because the tide was almost full. But instinct guided them, and it wasn't long before they were on the side of the rock, hidden from the cruiser, their eyes just peering over it.

"She is still in the cabin," George whispered. "She didn't go to sleep at all."

They waited another few moments, and then George stood up straight on the rock and shouted.

"Hey, lady! Hey, lady! Come out here, lady! We want to talk to you!"

They could feel the tense silence from the boat. Edwin and Conor kept their heads down. Conor put his hand softly over Babo's mouth, just in case.

"Do you hear me, lady," George called again. "Do you hear me?"

They saw the blurred movement in the cabin, and then they saw her coming to the side of the boat and staring over at George. She looked ghastly pale.

George blathered. This was the way he wanted to confuse her.

"Do you think I am a ghost, lady?" he taunted. "I'm not a ghost. You might be a ghost, but I'm not a ghost. See these hands? These are the hands that fixed the captain. Where's the captain? We put the hex on the captain. So what are you going to do now? You are on your own, you hear, and we'll fix you too. Hear that, lady? What are you going to do about it? You haven't much longer with the Yellow Ox. When we get the Yellow Ox we will bury him in the sea."

She did something.

She brought up the shotgun, which was near her hand, and she leveled it and she pulled the trigger. But before that happened, George was flat behind the rock. He put up his head again.

"Missed me," he jeered, and she fired again. They could hear the pellets rattling off the rock.

It was a double barrel, so now George rose to his feet and started to run toward the field.

She did what they hoped she would. She put two more cartridges into the gun from her pocket, came out of the boat, into the dinghy, and covered the few yards to the shore.

The boys couldn't see her, but they could hear her. She was muttering, and at times her voice rose to a whimper. It gave Conor the shivers to hear her.

She pulled up the dinghy and started to run, then she turned and, aiming the gun at the dinghy, pulled the trigger. The dinghy deflated. They could hear the rush of its deflation. Then she followed after George, screaming, "Captain! Captain!"

They counted ten and crawled out and over the rock.

They had counted on the dinghy. Now it was useless.

"You swim out," said Conor to Edwin. "I'll take Babo on my back."

Edwin didn't reply. He slid down to the water's edge and went in.

"Get on my back, Babo," said Conor. "Quick. Put your arms around my neck and tighten your legs around me, like riding a pony, you hear."

He felt the arms tight around his neck and the legs tight around his body and he slid down himself into the water.

It was shockingly cold. It made him gasp.

There were only about five yards between him and the floating cruiser, and already he saw Edwin clambering up the side and throwing himself in.

Babo's weight was sinking Conor. He had a job to keep his mouth over the water. Once he swallowed the sea. It had a terrible taste, but then his hands were at the side of the boat and Edwin was leaning over him and taking Babo off his back.

He held on to the boat for a second to get his breath back and to cough out the water and the nausea it had caused, and then with Edwin's help he was in and over.

"Quick! Quick!" said Edwin. "Throw off the ropes." He went to the stern himself, clambering over the galley, and Conor went up on the deck to the cleat where the front rope was tied.

It resisted him. It was very tight.

Now, almost panic-stricken, he got to his knees and wrestled with it, his wet clothes dripping on the deck. He had the little knife in his pocket, but he knew it would take ages.

Edwin came back to the cockpit. The gear lever was in neutral. He hesitated before he pressed the starter. Then he pressed it. It whirred and whirred. He was sure it would never start, that the sound of its whirring would bring the woman back. But suddenly it caught, a great, powerful roar.

He saw that Conor was still wrestling with the rope.

"Oh, hurry, Conor, hurry!" he called.

Conor gave a look to the land and saw the woman again. She was running back toward them again, waving the gun, her mouth open, calling, screaming at them.

He pushed and pulled and finally fell back as the rope left the cleat.

Edwin pushed the boat into reverse and it ran backward from the bay, farther and farther from the woman.

When he saw that he was a safe distance from the gun. Edwin put the engine into neutral, and then shot it into forward, and with a great surge the cruiser breasted into the lapping waves of the east wind of the morning.

Only then could he relax. He thought these last few minutes had been the longest his life had ever known or ever would know.

"We are free, Conor!" he called. "We are free! Free! Free!"

Conor was lying on his back on the deck where he had been thrown, just resting his palms flat on the boards, looking at the blue sky over his face, feeling the throbbing of the boards under his hands.

Then he sat up and went back and down into the cockpit.

Babo was sitting in a corner, wet and bewildered. Conor went to him.

"Listen, Babo," he said, "we are going home. Do you hear that? We are going home."

"I'm hungry," said Babo, getting up on his feet.

Conor laughed.

"You hear what he said, Edwin?" Conor asked. "He said he is hungry."

Edwin laughed.

"Oh, boy," he said. "What a kid! I hope old George got away." He headed the boat in a wide circle toward the cliff on the southeast side.

George had gotten away, but he hadn't gotten completely away.

When the captain heard the sound of the boat, he turned in his running and looked back and saw the woman running toward the bay. He followed after her, calling. His heart was surging. He knew the boys had gotten on the boat.

He called her. He saw her waving arms. He waited. He knew from the changing sound of the engine that the boat was free and away. He could have danced with joy, but he saw her turning back on him, and she turned back with determination.

So he put his hands on his chest and said, "Bet you can't hit me, lady." He was afraid she could. He was cut off a bit from the cliff. He knew he couldn't go there directly, so he ran for the left shore and she followed after him, calling despairingly, "Captain! Captain! Captain!"

The captain raised his chest and his arms to their fullest extent, swelled his breast and his muscles against the rope that held him down. He did that three times and knew he had the slack he needed. He pulled one of his arms from the bag. Now all he had to do was untie the rope at his chest and his feet.

He had done this almost as soon as the boys had left the tent, when he had come awake and aware of what had happened. He had fallen asleep with a mystery and now it was solved. What was missing? his mind had asked. And the answer was the broken pickax. The broken pickax, that was how they had gotten out.

He could have freed himself and run after them. He didn't.

Why didn't he?

It will have to be resolved this way, he thought. She would never have made that phone call. She never would have made that phone call. He knew this now. He knew it as well as if she had spoken to him. If she would do that, what would she do now? She wasn't herself. What she really needed was a doctor. It couldn't go on. It would have to end. They would be fugitives forever with the Yellow Ox. He knew that. You cannot murder four boys and hope that it will never be found out.

The captain did a strange thing.

He forced his free arms back into the bag under the rope.

And he thought of Agnes. And as he thought of her he became sad, and he had to crunch up his heavy face and his eyes so that he could keep himself from weeping for her as he heard her calling "Captain! Oh, Captain!" Later he had to tense all his muscles and clench his hands to stop himself from going to her.

She was bewildered.

Ever since she had known him all she had to do was call "Captain!" and there would be the captain at her side.

Now she called and she called and he did not come. It was a terrible thing for her.

But she followed the devil of a boy, down on the shore, stumbling over the rocks, falling on her knees, gashing her legs, cutting her hands with shells when she put them down to help herself to her feet. And all the time she was calling "Captain! Oh, Captain!" and the captain never came. But she persisted. She followed the boy on the shore and into the fields and over the stones and off the shore and back on the shore, and she knew she would hurt him when she saw him heading toward the cliff. Because from there he could go nowhere else. She wanted to hurt him. He was the embodiment of all her frustration and agony.

She got within range of him and she raised the gun, but she didn't fire, because, waving an arm at her in a last derisory gesture, the boy leapt from the cliff.

Below, he knew, were rocks, rocks, rocks, but he also knew the tide was full. Even when the tide was full they had seen the evil points of the rocks peeping over the water, but he picked what he thought was a smooth stretch and he jumped.

He had to wave his hands to keep his body from turning over. He had a lot of trouble keeping straight for that fifty feet, and then he was there, and he pinched his nostrils with one hand as he went under. Down, down, waiting for his body to jar against the rocks. But it didn't and before he had jumped he had seen the cruiser swinging in toward the cliff, and when he came up from below and shook the water from his eyes, he saw that it wasn't a dream, and the boat was coming toward him so he swam, with great joy, pausing now and again to shout, hearing them shouting back at him, and in no time at all their hands were reaching for him and he was lying in the cockpit.

chapter
20

George lay breathless for a while on the boards as they squatted close to him. They were overjoyed, but they found it hard to say anything.

"Glad you dropped in," said Edwin eventually, and this broke the tension. They all laughed and George got to his feet.

The engine of the boat was idling.

They looked back at the cliff.

They saw her up there. The soft wind was waving her hair. The sun was shining on her. She had her arms raised to the sky, and they could see that she was crying and hear that she was wailing. She made an odd spectacle. It made them feel uneasy, as if they had opened a forbidden door and looked at something they weren't supposed to see.

"Let's go, skipper," said George suddenly. "Come on

and give her the gun. Let's go home and face the music."

Edwin put the engine into gear, and opened up the throttle and swung the cruiser around in a wide arc, heading in toward the bay. The waves were small, barely disturbing the top of the sea, but the way they slapped against the bow seemed to them like the joyful clappings of hands.

"You take the wheel now, Conor," said Edwin. "We don't want to pile her on a rock at this stage."

So Conor took the wheel and gazed ahead and picked out the well-known landmarks and headed the boat for home. They would be about an hour getting there, he knew, even with the power of the engine.

George had been looking into the cabin.

The Yellow Ox was gazing out at him.

"I don't like that fellow," said George. "Let's get him out of there. Let's get him up on the deck. How about it?"

"Right," said Edwin.

So they went into the cabin and looked at the ox. The lady had polished him. He was brightly burnished. They looked at the bracelets and bangles, the pin and the necklaces. She had cleaned those. Parts of them were bad, but most of them were very good, the tiny colored enamel pieces and the gold were beautiful.

Edwin wrapped them up in the handkerchief and tied the ends with two knots.

Then they approached the Yellow Ox.

They were strangely reluctant to handle him, as if he

would burst into action and charge them the minute they placed a finger on him. Now that he was cleaned you could see the great chest and the folds around the powerful neck.

"Right," said George, "let's go," and he caught the back part of him. Edwin caught the front part, and they lifted him off the table. They nearly fell when the full weight of him came on their arms, but they got him out of the cabin and, resting in the cockpit, they counted one two three as if he were a sack of potatoes and elevated him up to the deck.

Then they climbed on the deck and pushed him until he was above the skylight and facing the way that they were going.

"Like a figurehead," said George.

"Very few boats have figureheads like that," said Edwin.

"Where's Babo?" George asked.

"Hey, Conor, where's Babo?" Edwin asked.

"Where do you think?" Conor asked, grinning. "He's in the galley there, stealing food."

George slapped his thigh.

"That's the Babo," he said. "You know, I look at us now, and never in the history of boats have there been three such bedraggled characters like us manning a good ship."

They looked at one another and they laughed. Their clothes were wet and torn so that you could see parts of a leg and a chest and a back and a stomach.

"Just wait until our parents see us," said Edwin.

Conor frowned.

"They'll murder us," he said. "And it was all my fault."

"Ah, come on," said George. "Don't start on that chorus again. They'll be so glad to see us that they won't remember what happened until it's all over." He jumped down from the deck.

"Hey, Babo! Babo!" he called. "Come on out and see the fresh air." He opened the galley door. Babo was sitting on the floor solemnly eating an apple. George got on his knees in front of him.

"Come on, Babo," he said. "Don't you want to see? Come on and get up on the deck and see yourself coming home."

Babo nodded, so George lifted him and brought him out and put him up on the deck. Babo surveyed the deck. Then he saw the Yellow Ox shining and gleaming in the morning sun and he walked up to it, pointed at it, and turned back to them.

"Nice hobbyhorse," said Babo, and catching one horn of the ox he sat astride him and started joggling to and fro.

Edwin was laughing.

"Look at that!" he said. "Babo makes a hobbyhorse out of the Yellow Ox and he frightens the life out of the rest of us."

Then they heard the sound of the helicopter. It was coming straight up the bay toward them, just a small dot now in the sky. They were overjoyed. They started jumping and waving their arms.

The helicopter wasn't going to come near them, but Joe saw the flashing from the front of the boat and the waving arms.

"Pat! Pat!" he said. "Look at that boat. Go on over it."

"What's wrong with it?" Pat asked.

"They are waving from it," said Joe. He put the binoculars up to his eyes and focused them.

"You won't believe me, Pat," he said, "but there are three and a half boys on that boat and they are trying to throw their arms at us."

"You're fooling," said Pat. "It couldn't be them!"

"But it is them! It is them!" said Joe in great excitement. "It has to be them. Go down, can't you. Go down so we can have a look at them."

Pat did so. He dived low toward the approaching boat, and when he got near enough he circled widely around it. Even he could see that there were three boys and a half boy on the boat. It was the craziest thing he had ever seen, the little fellow in front sitting on some sort of a thing that was reflecting the rays of the sun like a hundred mirrors.

Joe was leaning out of the window, waving like mad.

"Hello, fellows!" he was calling. "Hello, fellows!" as if they could hear him over the sound of the two engines.

"Isn't it marvelous?" he was asking Pat, shouting it back at him. "Isn't it wonderful? There they are. What did I tell you about having hope? What did I tell you, you mechanized Scrooge, about having hope?"

But Pat wasn't listening to him. He was shouting into the radio speaker.

"Yes, it's them. We are looking at them. I don't know how and I don't know where, but they are not dead. They are right down under me now, driving an expensive cruiser. Yes, yes! Blond, brown, and dark and a small towhead. I can't be mistaken, I tell you. These are they. Break out the flags. Tell all the parents. Think of it! All those parents off our backs. Right out. They're safe. They are on their way. They look all right. We are taking off. Hope we never have to see you again. Good-bye. Take over from here."

"Now, how about the boat from Australia?" asked Joe.

"Don't be silly," said Pat. "I can tell you that's a great load off my mind." He leaned out the window and waved, and shouted too, although he knew they couldn't hear him.

"So long, fellows," he called. "And next time stay away from the sea."

They saw the helocopter jump upward, bounce a little, as if the pilot were making it dance, and then it whirred away from them, zooming joyfully.

They were excited and laughing at the antics of the helicopter as they saw it disappearing toward the mainland.

"Now they will all know," said Edwin.

And indeed the word of their homecoming spread like a heather fire on a hillside in the drought of the summer.

Nobody wants to be thinking of four boys' bodies drifting at the bottom of the sea. Or searching for them day after day along the shore. Nobody wants to come upon the drowned body of a boy amid the wrack of the sea. Nobody wanted this, and yet there were very few who did not believe that the boys had drowned. Very few. If a fisherman died in the sea, this was expected. You looked for him and found him and buried him. But not these boys. The sight of the haggard parents under such a strain—to be suddenly freed of it! This was like a miracle. What? It isn't so? It cannot be? You don't mean it? And they grabbed for their hats or their caps or their bicycles or their vans or their horses or their automobiles or went on shanks' mare, and started flowing down to the pier, leaving the cornfields and the hayfields and the turf bogs and the hotel and the sunbathing and the swimming and the dinner to be burned in the pot or the stove or the great electric kitchen. From all sides they came, running and calling.

The boys saw the first of it about half an hour later as they were easing the boat toward the shore. People running along the roads. Some of them stopping to stand on a rock or wave a scarf or a shirt or a hat, tiny figures on the headlands. They saw them running down the hillsides, and along the single road they saw cars raising clouds of dust, all of them converging on the big pier near the sandy shore, as if they were being drawn by colored strings.

The boys just stood and stared.

"I see them! I see them!" said George. "Look! Look! They have stopped the car."

You couldn't mistake the car. It was an American model, a huge, long one in comparison with all the others.

George was on deck, waving. He could see the binoculars his father was holding. So he waved and waved, jumping up and down.

Edwin saw his father's car on the road too, bowling along in a dust cloud and seeming to be growing arms out of the windows.

Conor had to keep his eye on the land ahead of him, so he couldn't look, but he knew that his father and his mother and his brothers and sisters would be pelting down to that pier, foot-on-high, as they say.

It was a marvelous sight, it really was. It blotted out all that had happened to them. It was nearly worthwhile, they were thinking, to see this, as if the land were putting on a colorful spectacle for their benefit.

Because it was colorful. It was a riot of color as the streams converged on the road to the pier, on the pier, all over the shelter wall of the pier, white and red and orange and blue and indigo, all the colors of the rainbow were being waved and worn by the converging mass; and as they got closer to the pier, they seemed to be engulfed in an enormous wave of sustained sound that was even drowning out the sound of the engine of the boat.

And this sound swelled to an enormous shout as they distinguished the figure of little Babo, sitting on the Yellow Ox, holding a horn with one hand and finishing the core of an apple with the other one.

A great gob, an explosion of color, sound, cheering, ruffled the vault of the sky.

And the boys just stood and looked, speechless, and only Conor could think at all, and he thought, I wonder will I ever see George and Edwin again?

I hope I will, he thought. I hope I will, as he steered the boat into the vortex of welcome, and toward his mother, who was standing dangerously near the end of the pier, her arms held out, calling, "Babo! Babo! Babo!"

About the author

Walter Macken was born in Galway, Ireland. He spent most of his life in the theater and acted in, produced, and designed more than one hundred plays for the Galway Gaelic Theatre and the Abbey Theatre company. In 1952 he acted on Broadway in his own play, *Home Is the Hero*.

His first novel was published in 1948, and from then on he had a novel, play, or book of short stories published every year until his death in 1967.

Walter Macken is the author of one other book for children, *The Flight of the Doves*.